P9-CLV-741

STRANGER THINGS

ZOMBIE BOYS #1

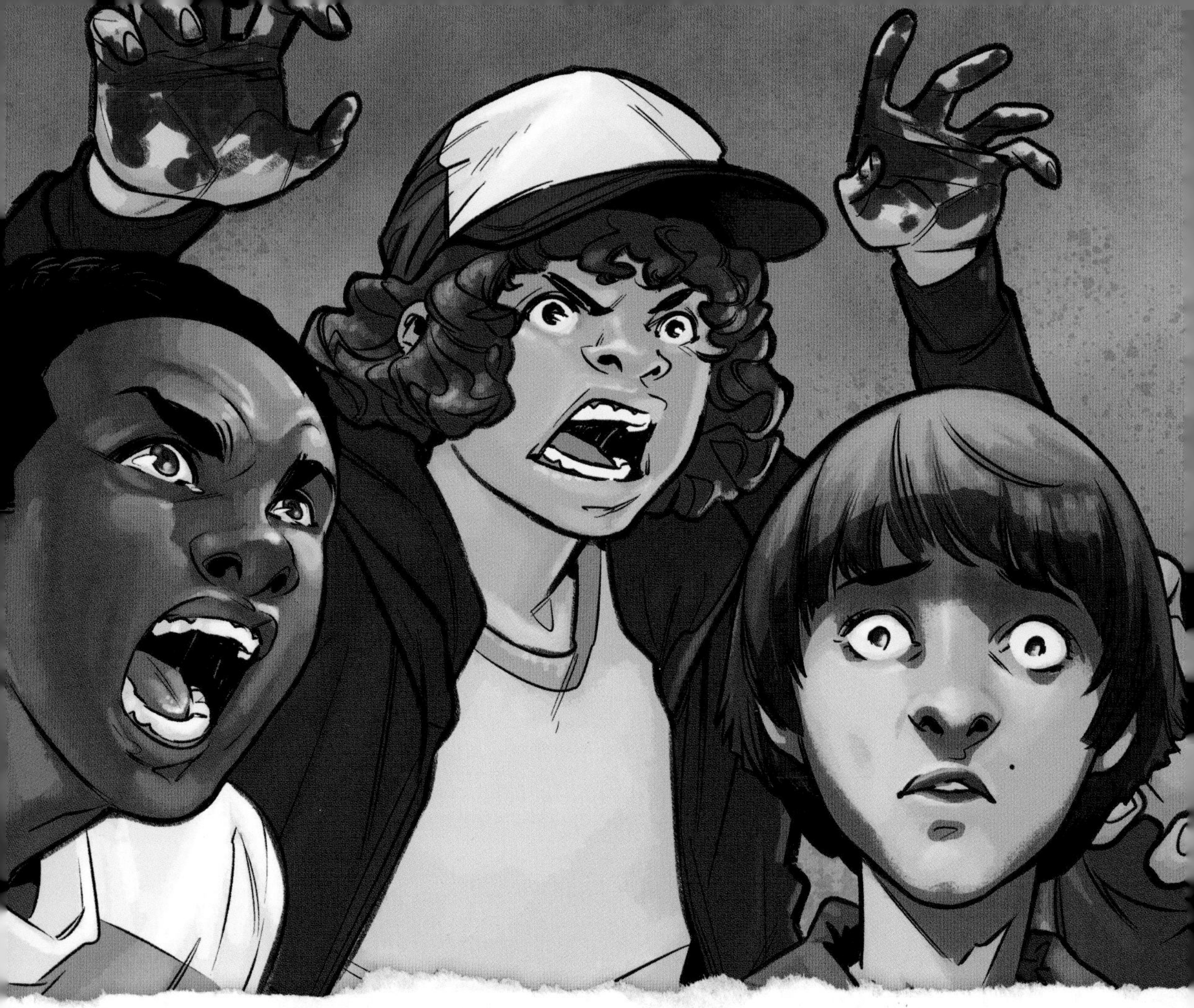

STRANGER THINGS™

ZOMBIE BOYS #1

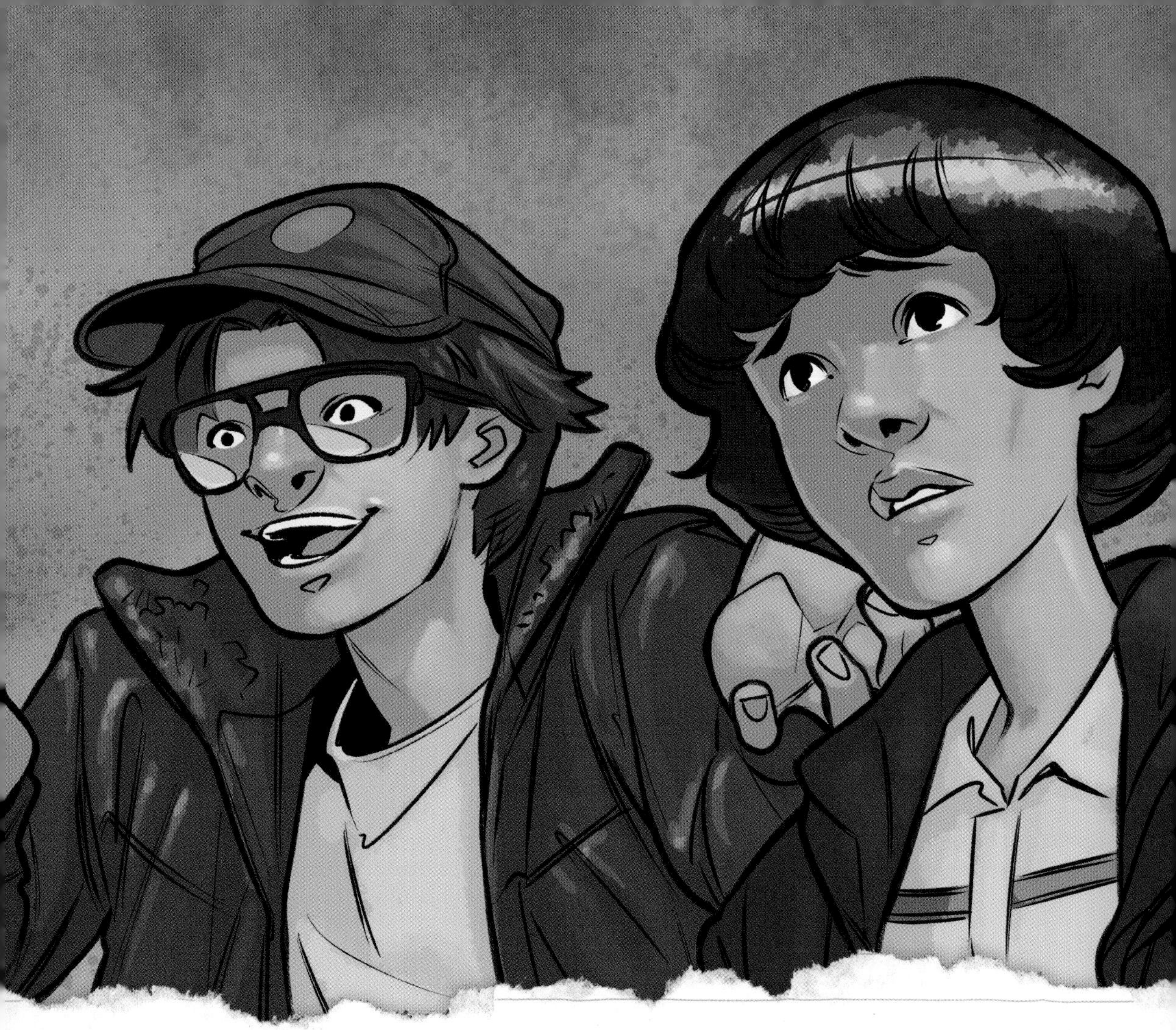

script by
GREG PAK

Art by
VALERIA FAVOCCIA

colors by
DAN JACKSON

Lettering by
NATE PIEKOS OF BLAMBOT®

cover Art by
RON CHAN

ABDO Spotlight
DARK HORSE BOOKS

ABDOBOOKS.COM

Reinforced library bound edition published in 2022 by Spotlight, a division of ABDO, PO Box 398166, Minneapolis, Minnesota 55439. Spotlight produces high-quality reinforced library bound editions for schools and libraries.
Published by agreement with Dark Horse Comics.

Printed in the United States of America, North Mankato, Minnesota.
092021
012022

THIS BOOK CONTAINS
RECYCLED MATERIALS

NETFLIX
OFFICIAL MERCHANDISE
©NETFLIX

Library of Congress Control Number: 2021939399

Publisher's Cataloging-in-Publication Data

Names: Pak, Greg, author. | Favoccia, Valeria; Jackson, Dan; Piekos, Nate, illustrators.
Title: Zombie Boys / writers: Greg Pak; art: Valeria Favoccia; Dan Jackson; and Nate Piekos.
Description: Minneapolis, Minnesota: Spotlight, 2022 | Series: Stranger Things
Summary: When a new kid to the AV club wants to make a zombie movie based on Will's drawings, the boys come to terms with the real horrors they've already faced.
Identifiers: ISBN 9781098250782 (#1, lib. bdg.) | ISBN 9781098250799 (#2, lib. bdg.) | ISBN 9781098250805 (#3, lib. bdg.)
Subjects: LCSH: Stranger things (Television program)--Juvenile fiction. | Science fiction television programs--Juvenile fiction. | Supernatural disappearances--Juvenile fiction. | Monsters--Juvenile fiction. | Zombies--Juvenile fiction. | Graphic novels--Juvenile fiction
Classification: DDC 741.5--dc23

Spotlight

A Division of ABDO
abdobooks.com

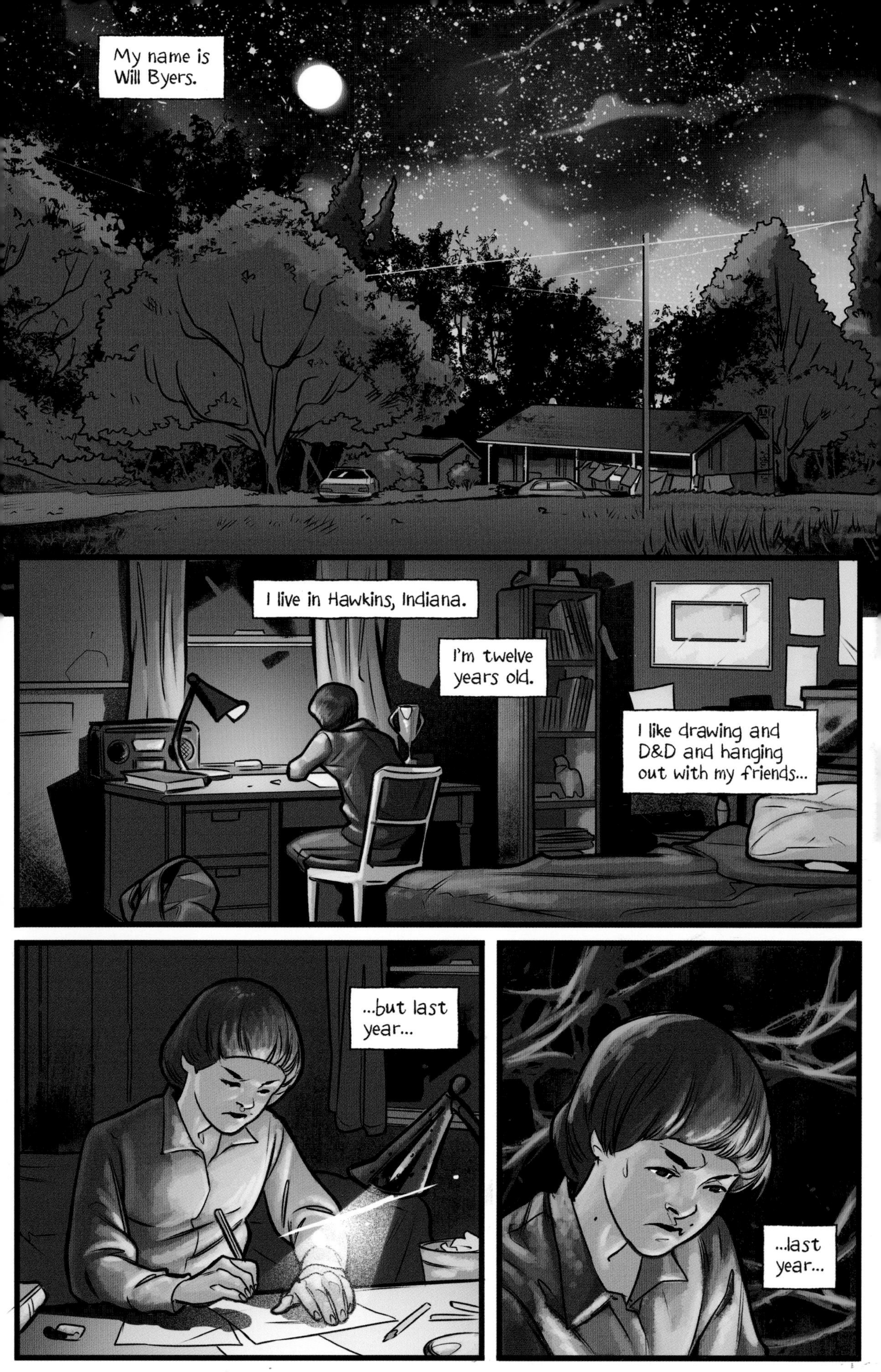
My name is Will Byers.
I live in Hawkins, Indiana.
I'm twelve years old.
I like drawing and D&D and hanging out with my friends...
...but last year...
...last year...

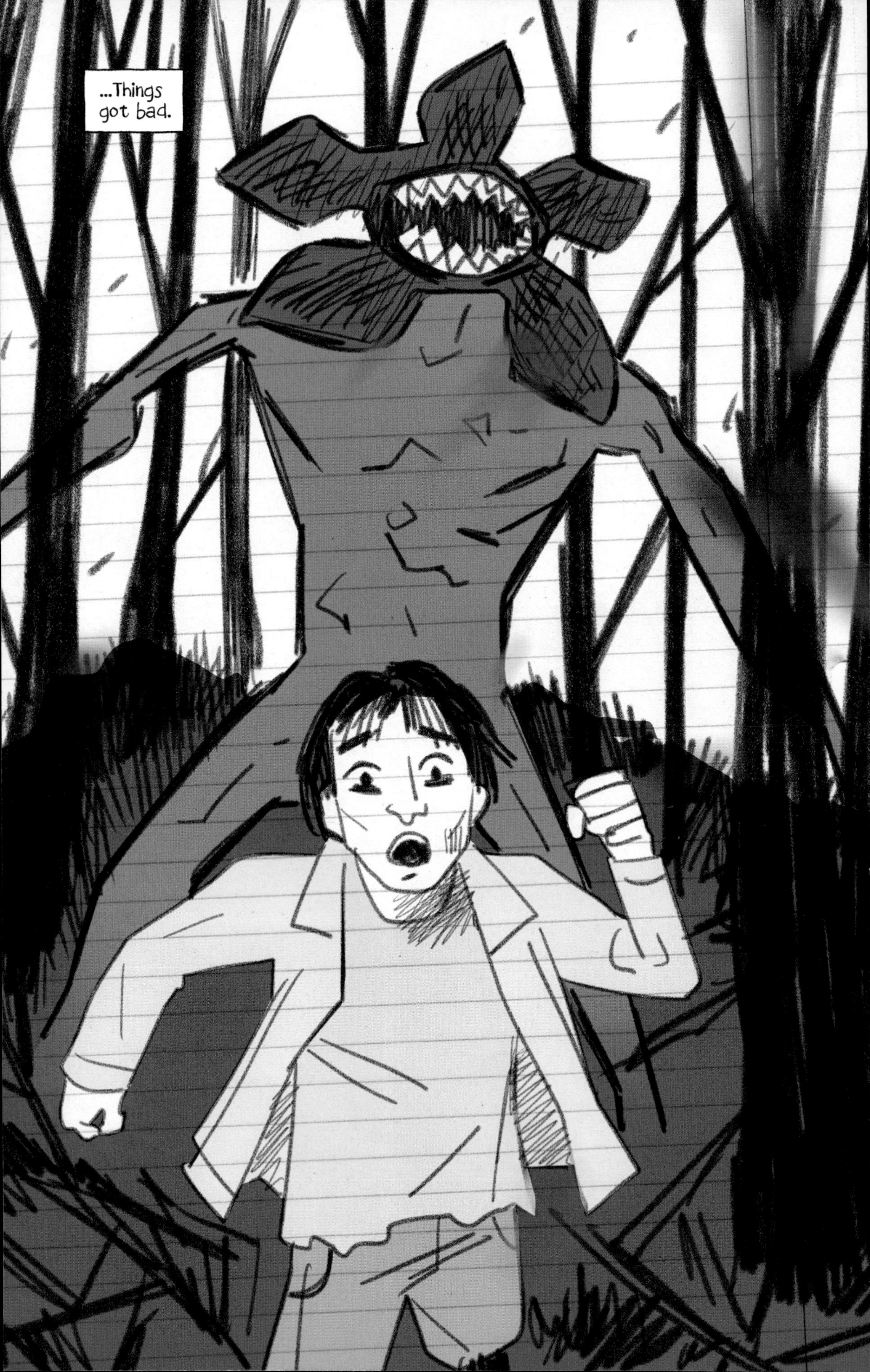
...Things got bad.

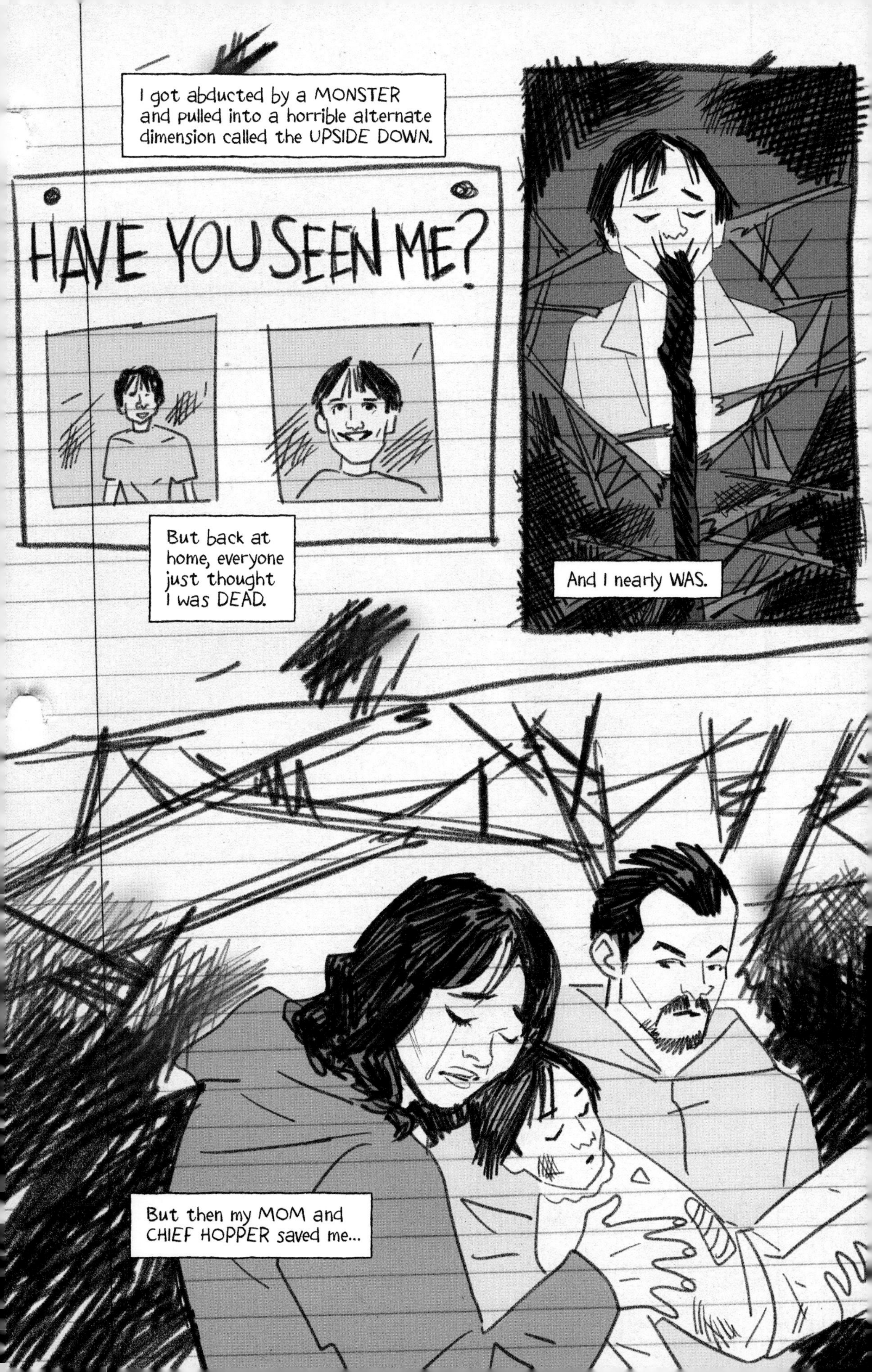
I got abducted by a MONSTER and pulled into a horrible alternate dimension called the UPSIDE DOWN.
HAVE YOU SEEN ME?
But back at home, everyone just thought I was DEAD.
And I nearly WAS.
But then my MOM and CHIEF HOPPER saved me...

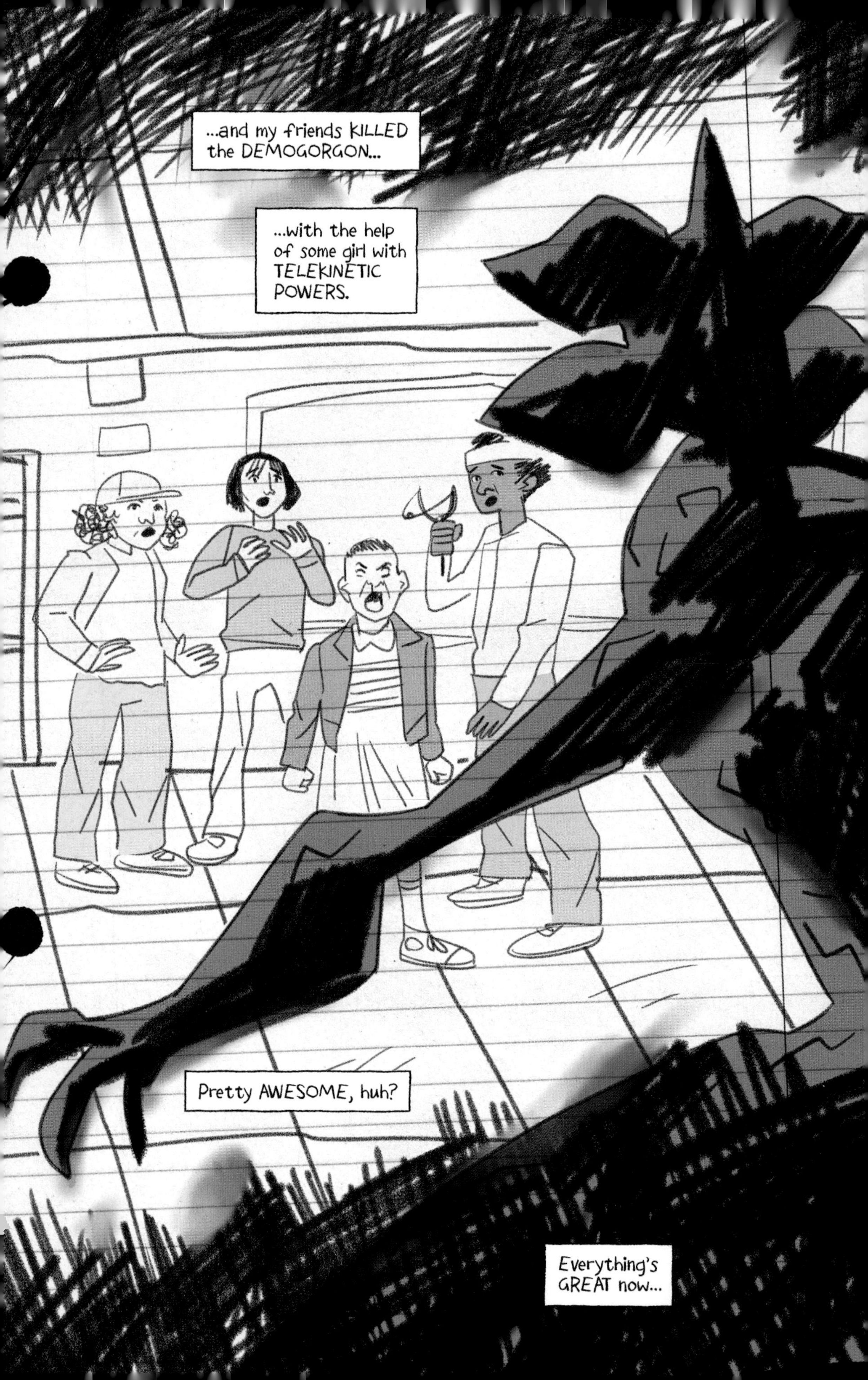
...and my friends KILLED the DEMOGORGON...
...with the help of some girl with TELEKINETIC POWERS.
Pretty AWESOME, huh?
Everything's GREAT now...

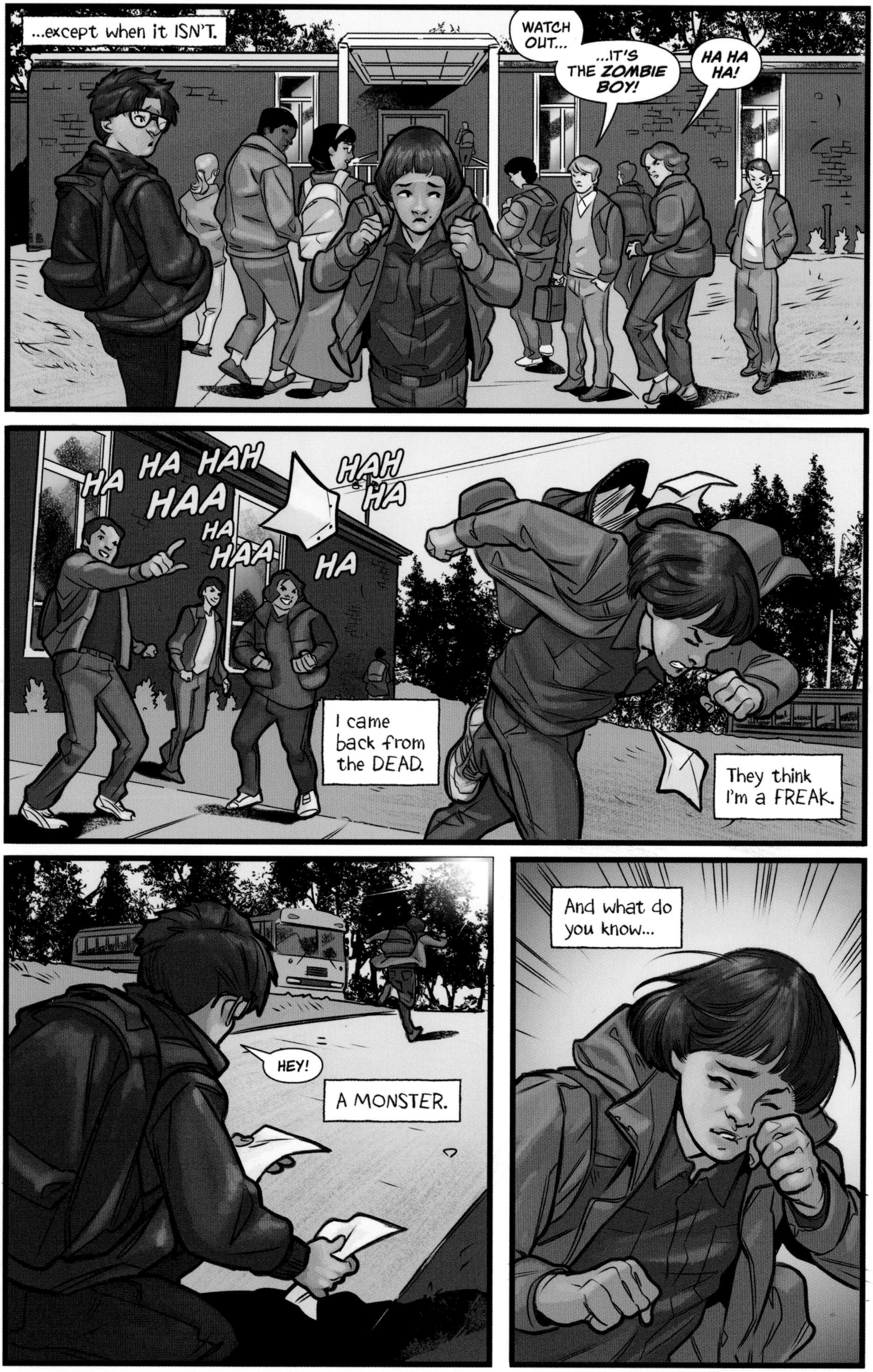
...except when it ISN'T.
WATCH OUT...
...IT'S THE ZOMBIE BOY!
HA HA HA!
HA HA HAH HAA HA HAA
HAH HA
HA
I came back from the DEAD.
They think I'm a FREAK.
HEY!
A MONSTER.
And what do you know...

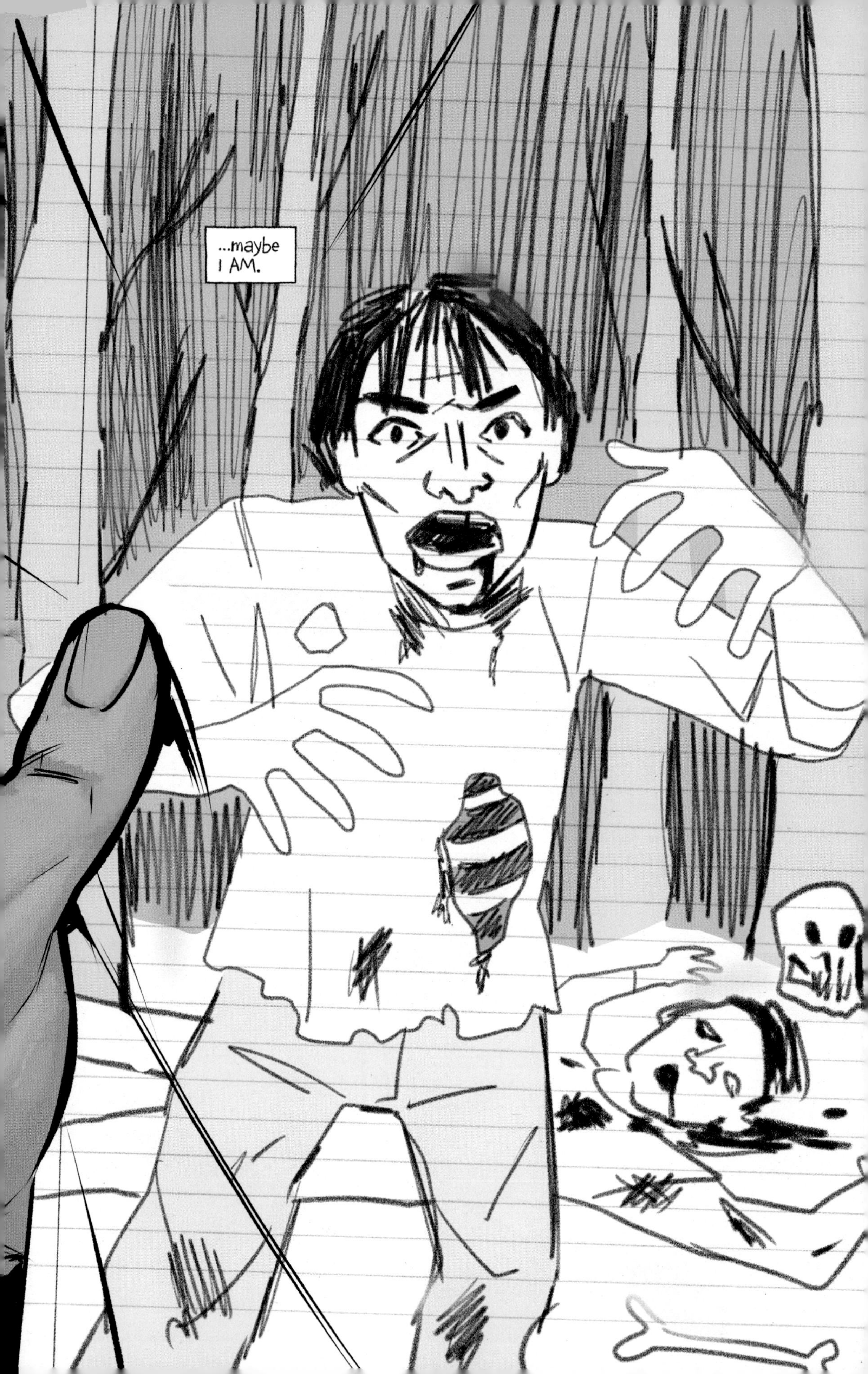
...maybe I AM.

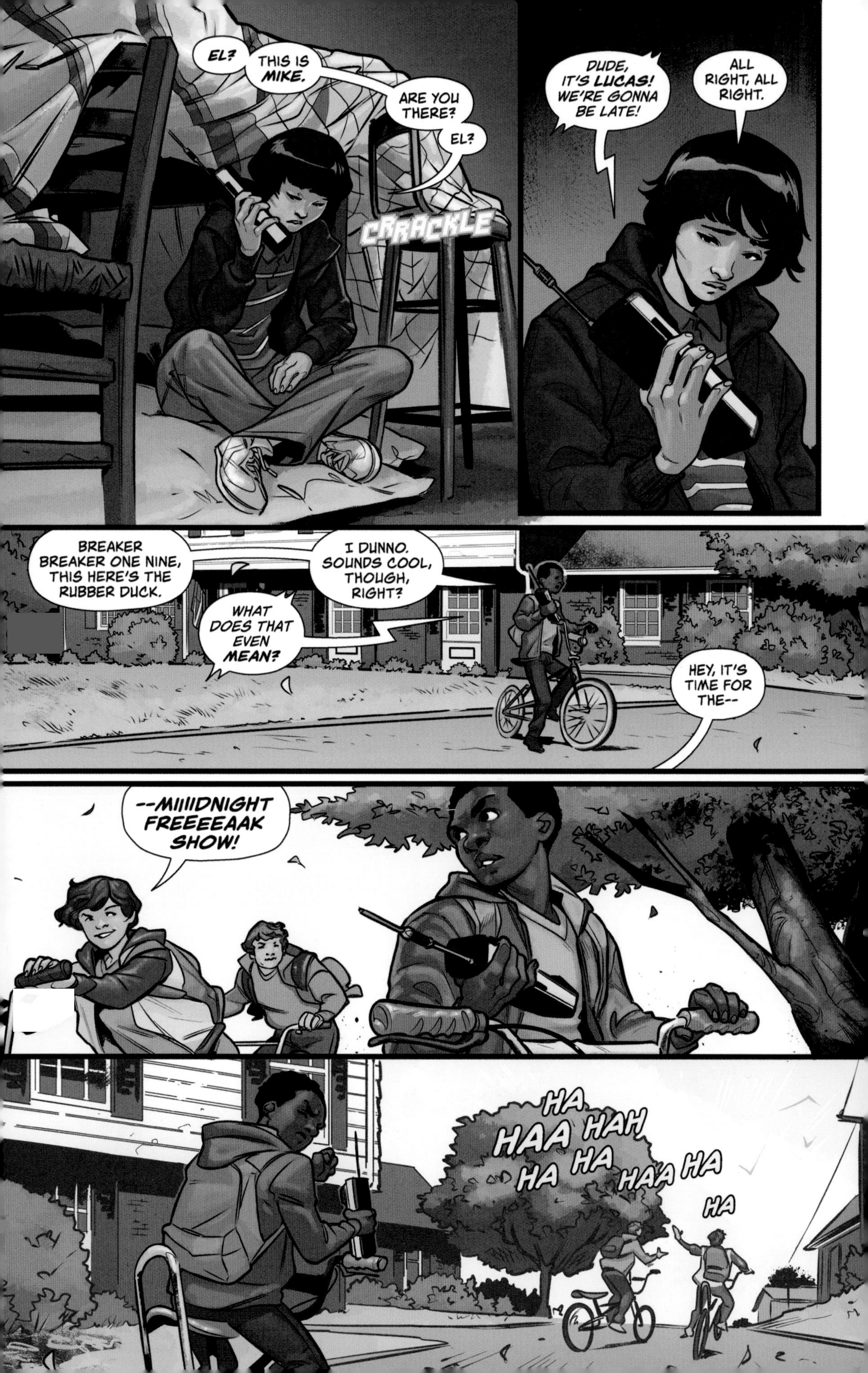
EL?
THIS IS MIKE.
ARE YOU THERE?
EL?
CRRACKLE
DUDE, IT'S LUCAS! WE'RE GONNA BE LATE!
ALL RIGHT, ALL RIGHT.
BREAKER BREAKER ONE NINE, THIS HERE'S THE RUBBER DUCK.
WHAT DOES THAT EVEN MEAN?
I DUNNO. SOUNDS COOL, THOUGH, RIGHT?
HEY, IT'S TIME FOR THE--
--MIIIIDNIGHT FREEEEAAK SHOW!
HA
HAA HAH
HA HA
HAA HA
HA

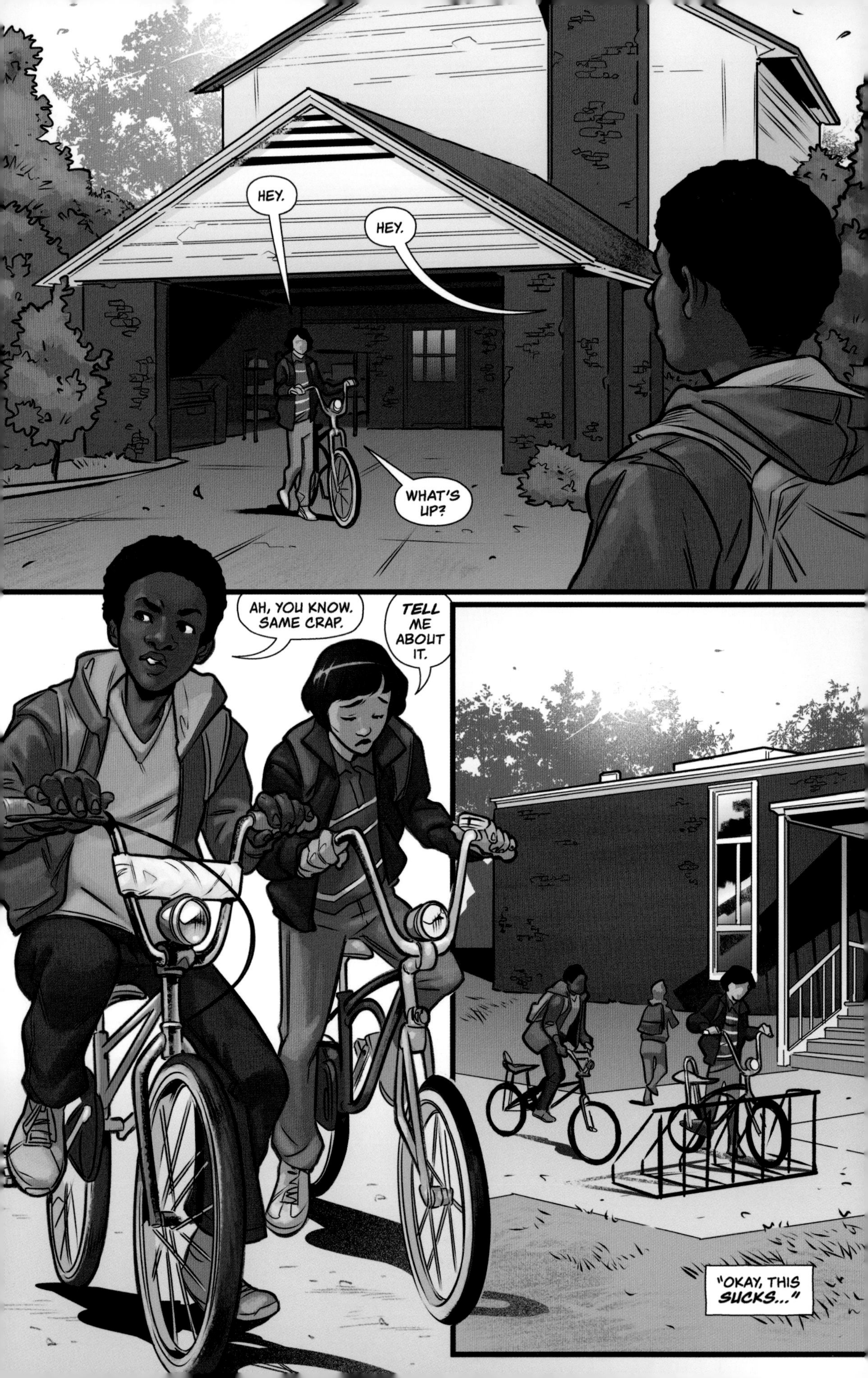
HEY.
HEY.
WHAT'S UP?
AH, YOU KNOW. SAME CRAP.
TELL ME ABOUT IT.
"OKAY, THIS SUCKS..."

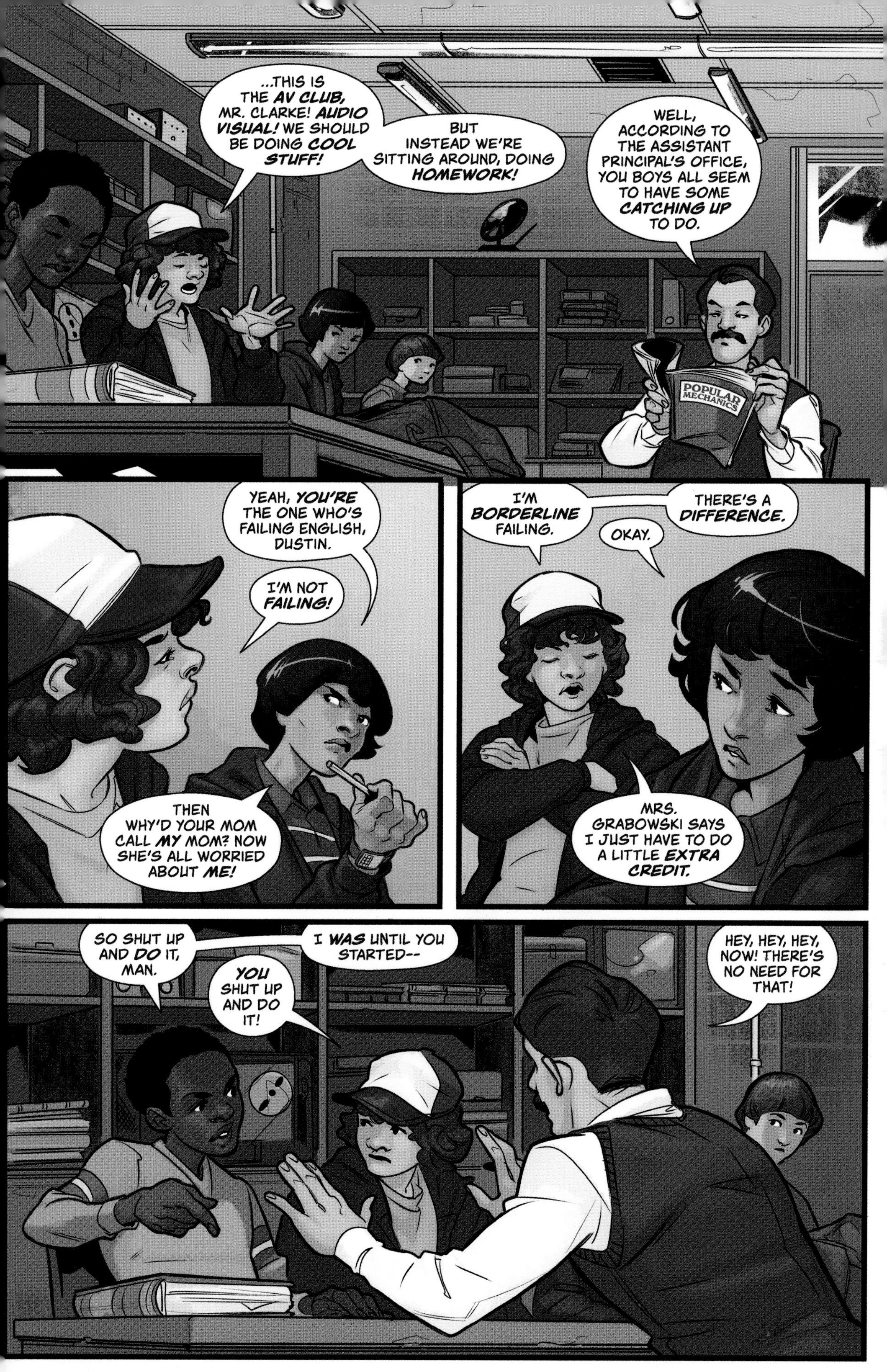
...THIS IS THE AV CLUB, MR. CLARKE! AUDIO VISUAL! WE SHOULD BE DOING COOL STUFF!
BUT INSTEAD WE'RE SITTING AROUND, DOING HOMEWORK!
WELL, ACCORDING TO THE ASSISTANT PRINCIPAL'S OFFICE, YOU BOYS ALL SEEM TO HAVE SOME CATCHING UP TO DO.
POPULAR MECHANICS
YEAH, YOU'RE THE ONE WHO'S FAILING ENGLISH, DUSTIN.
I'M NOT FAILING!
THEN WHY'D YOUR MOM CALL MY MOM? NOW SHE'S ALL WORRIED ABOUT ME!
I'M BORDERLINE FAILING.
THERE'S A DIFFERENCE.
OKAY.
MRS. GRABOWSKI SAYS I JUST HAVE TO DO A LITTLE EXTRA CREDIT.
SO SHUT UP AND DO IT, MAN.
I WAS UNTIL YOU STARTED--
YOU SHUT UP AND DO IT!
HEY, HEY, HEY, NOW! THERE'S NO NEED FOR THAT!

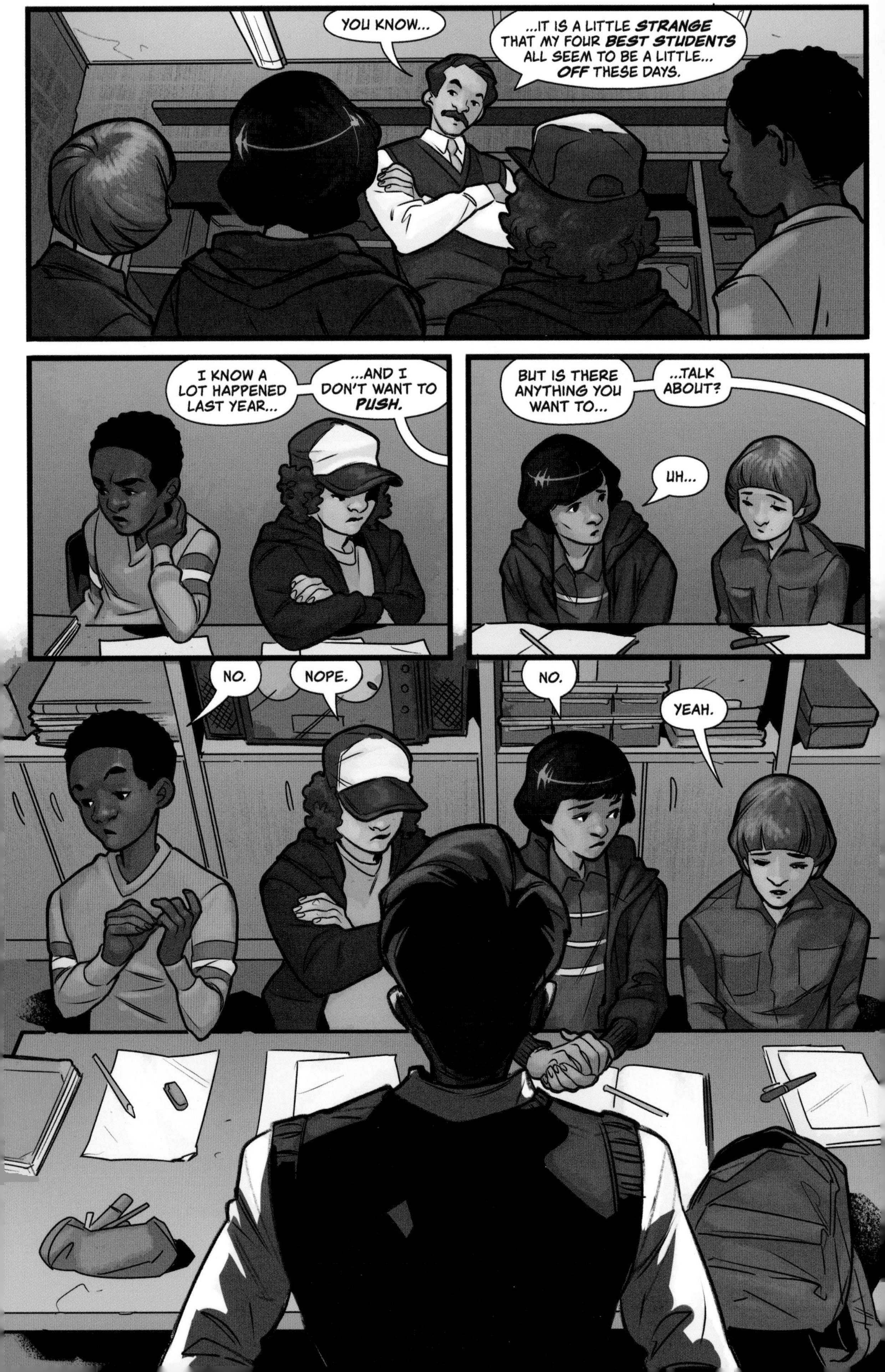
YOU KNOW...
...IT IS A LITTLE STRANGE THAT MY FOUR BEST STUDENTS ALL SEEM TO BE A LITTLE... OFF THESE DAYS.
I KNOW A LOT HAPPENED LAST YEAR...
...AND I DON'T WANT TO PUSH.
BUT IS THERE ANYTHING YOU WANT TO...
...TALK ABOUT?
UH...
NO.
NOPE.
NO.
YEAH.

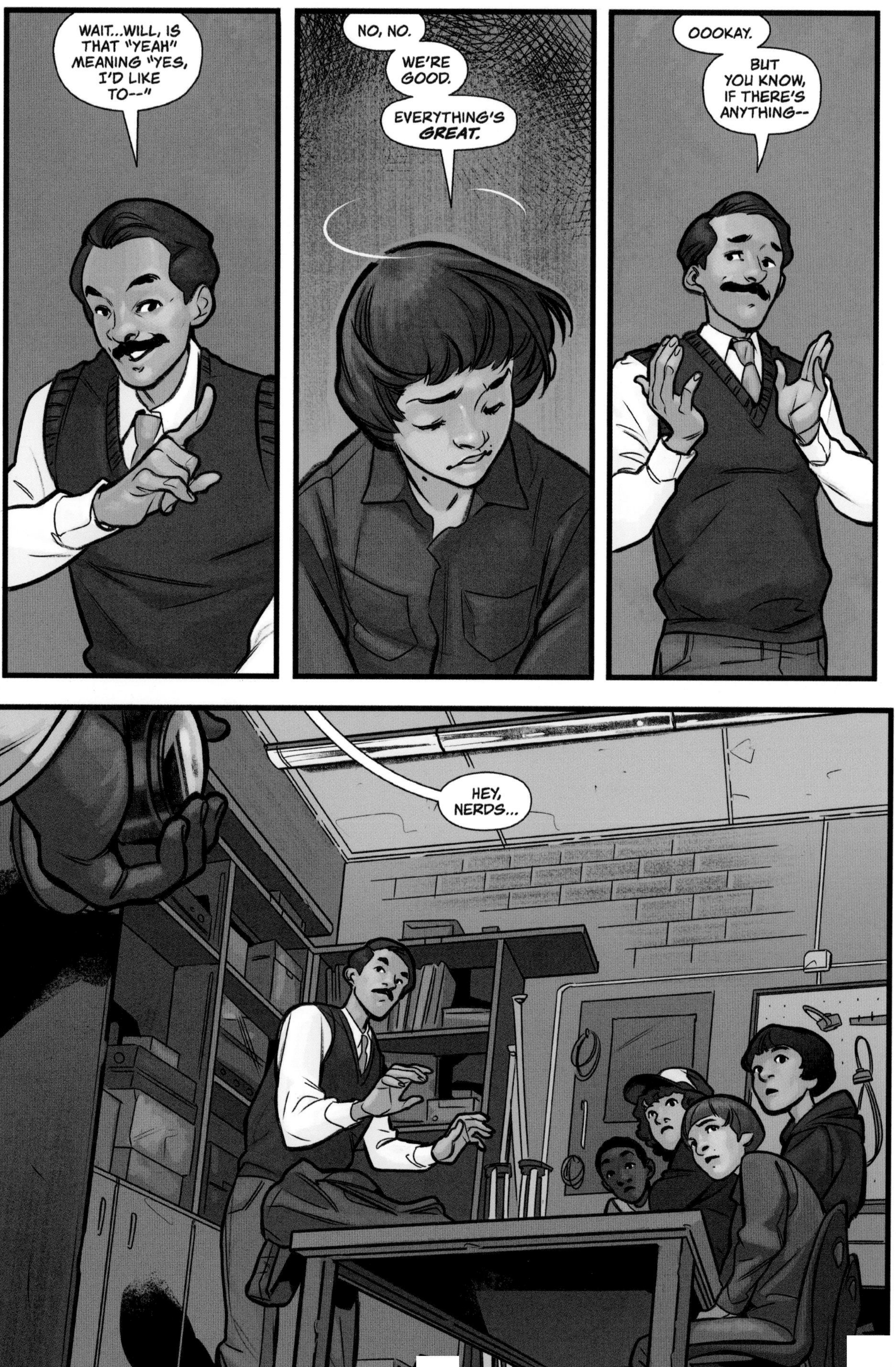
WAIT...WILL, IS THAT "YEAH" MEANING "YES, I'D LIKE TO--"
NO, NO.
WE'RE GOOD.
EVERYTHING'S *GREAT.*
OOOKAY.
BUT YOU KNOW, IF THERE'S ANYTHING--
HEY, NERDS...

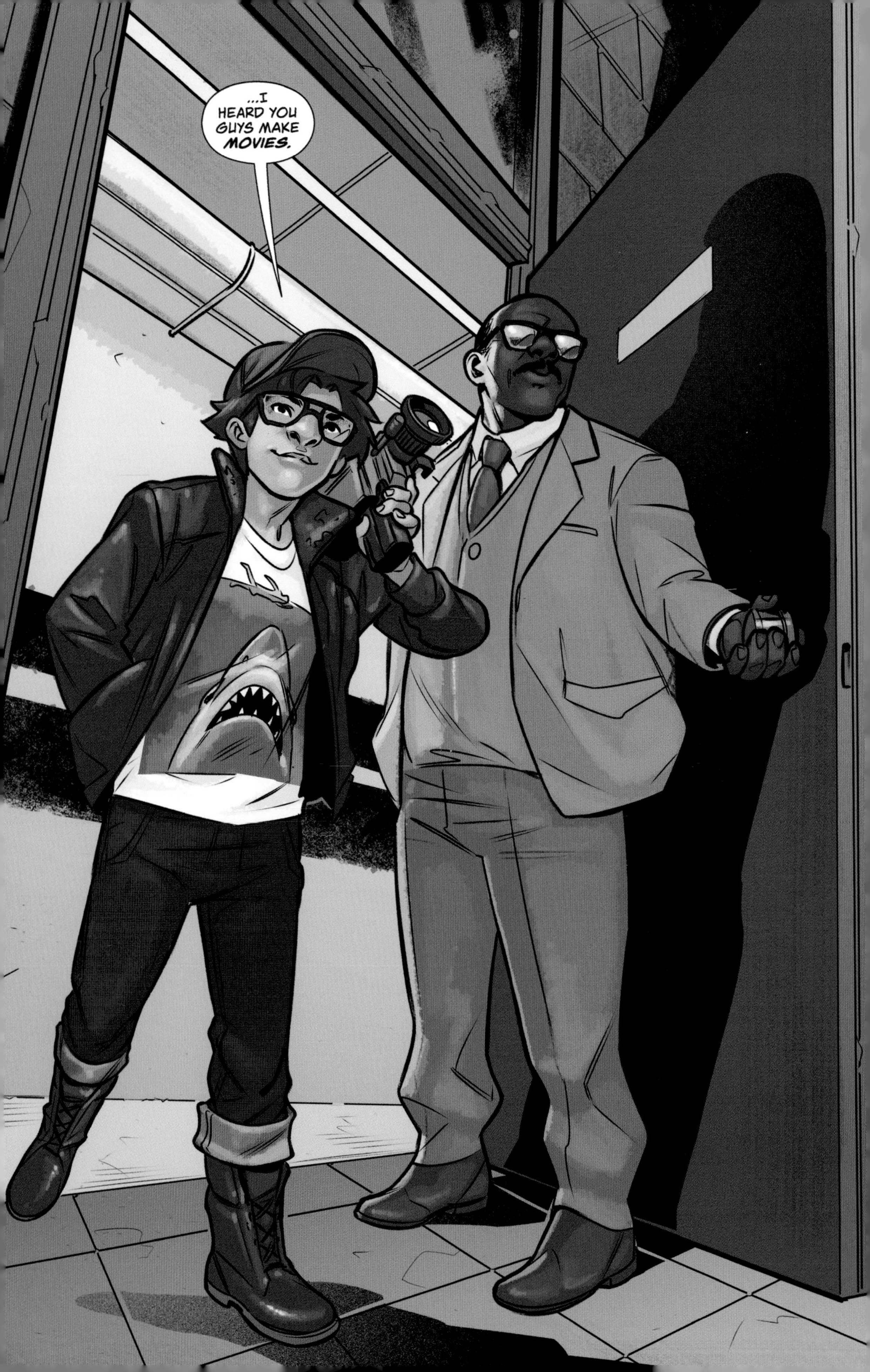
...I HEARD YOU GUYS MAKE MOVIES.

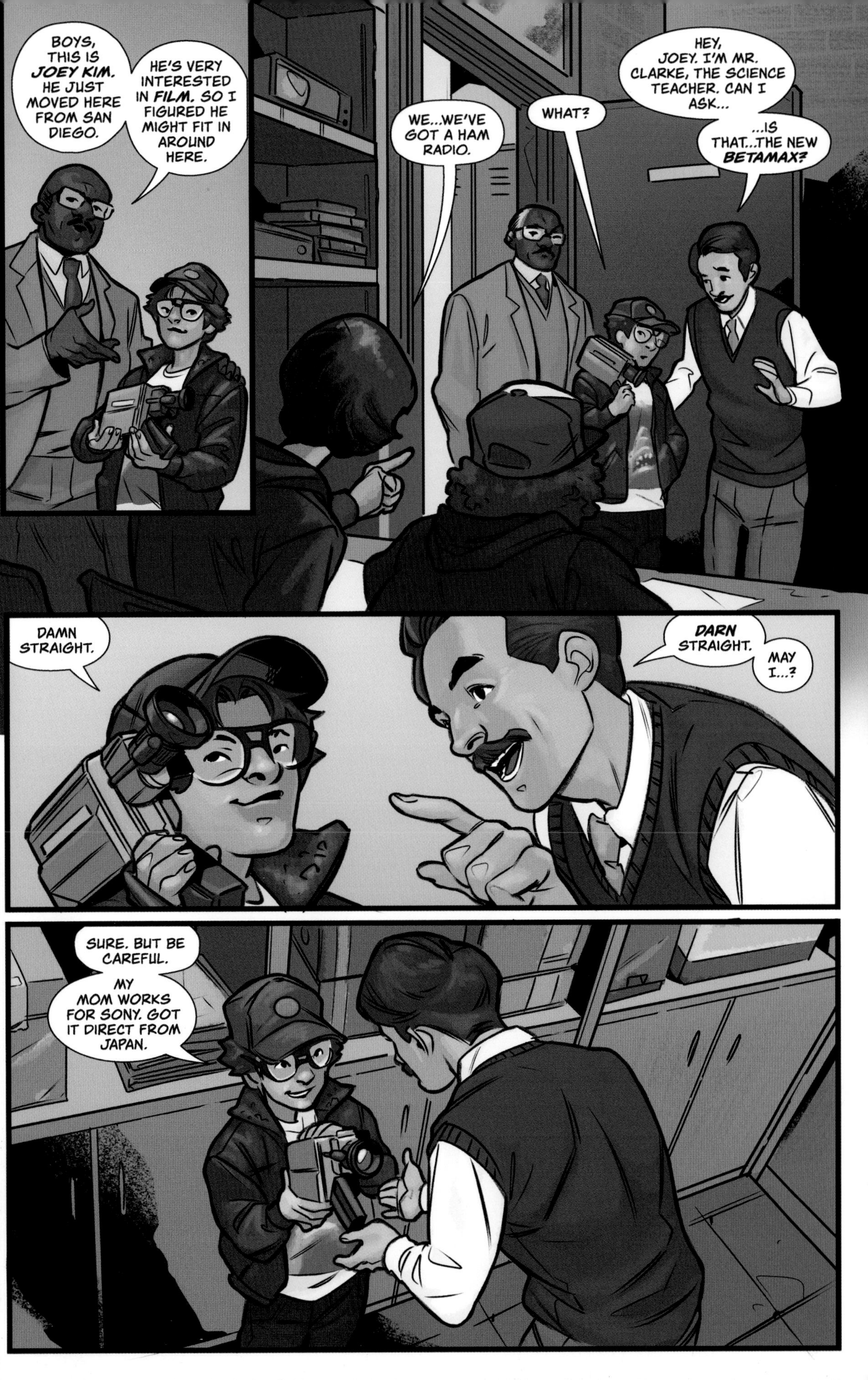
BOYS, THIS IS JOEY KIM. HE JUST MOVED HERE FROM SAN DIEGO.
HE'S VERY INTERESTED IN FILM. SO I FIGURED HE MIGHT FIT IN AROUND HERE.
WE...WE'VE GOT A HAM RADIO.
WHAT?
HEY, JOEY. I'M MR. CLARKE, THE SCIENCE TEACHER. CAN I ASK...
...IS THAT...THE NEW BETAMAX?
DAMN STRAIGHT.
DARN STRAIGHT.
MAY I...?
SURE. BUT BE CAREFUL.
MY MOM WORKS FOR SONY. GOT IT DIRECT FROM JAPAN.

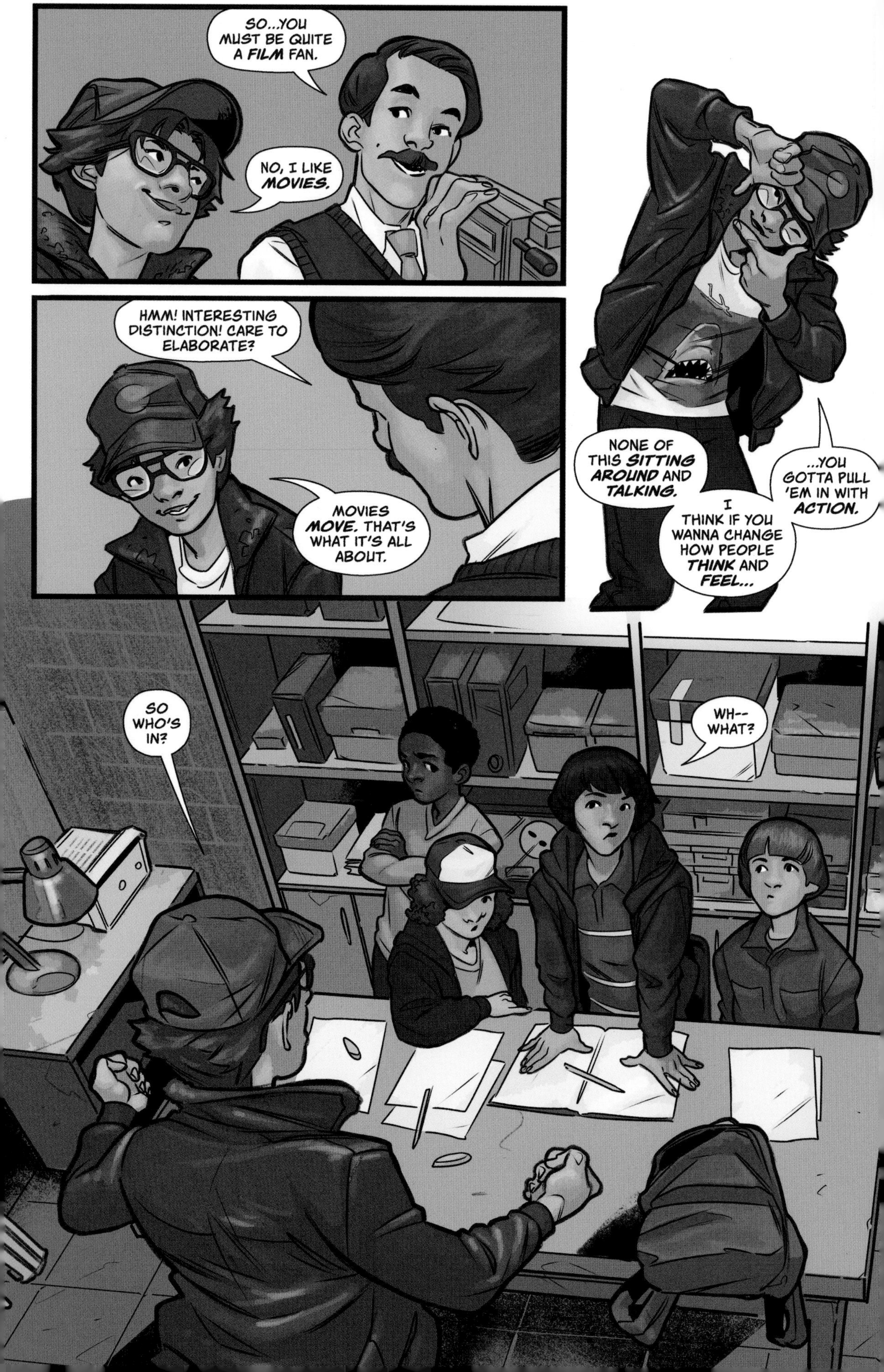
SO...YOU MUST BE QUITE A FILM FAN.
NO, I LIKE MOVIES.
HMM! INTERESTING DISTINCTION! CARE TO ELABORATE?
MOVIES MOVE. THAT'S WHAT IT'S ALL ABOUT.
NONE OF THIS SITTING AROUND AND TALKING.
I THINK IF YOU WANNA CHANGE HOW PEOPLE THINK AND FEEL...
...YOU GOTTA PULL 'EM IN WITH ACTION.
SO WHO'S IN?
WH-- WHAT?

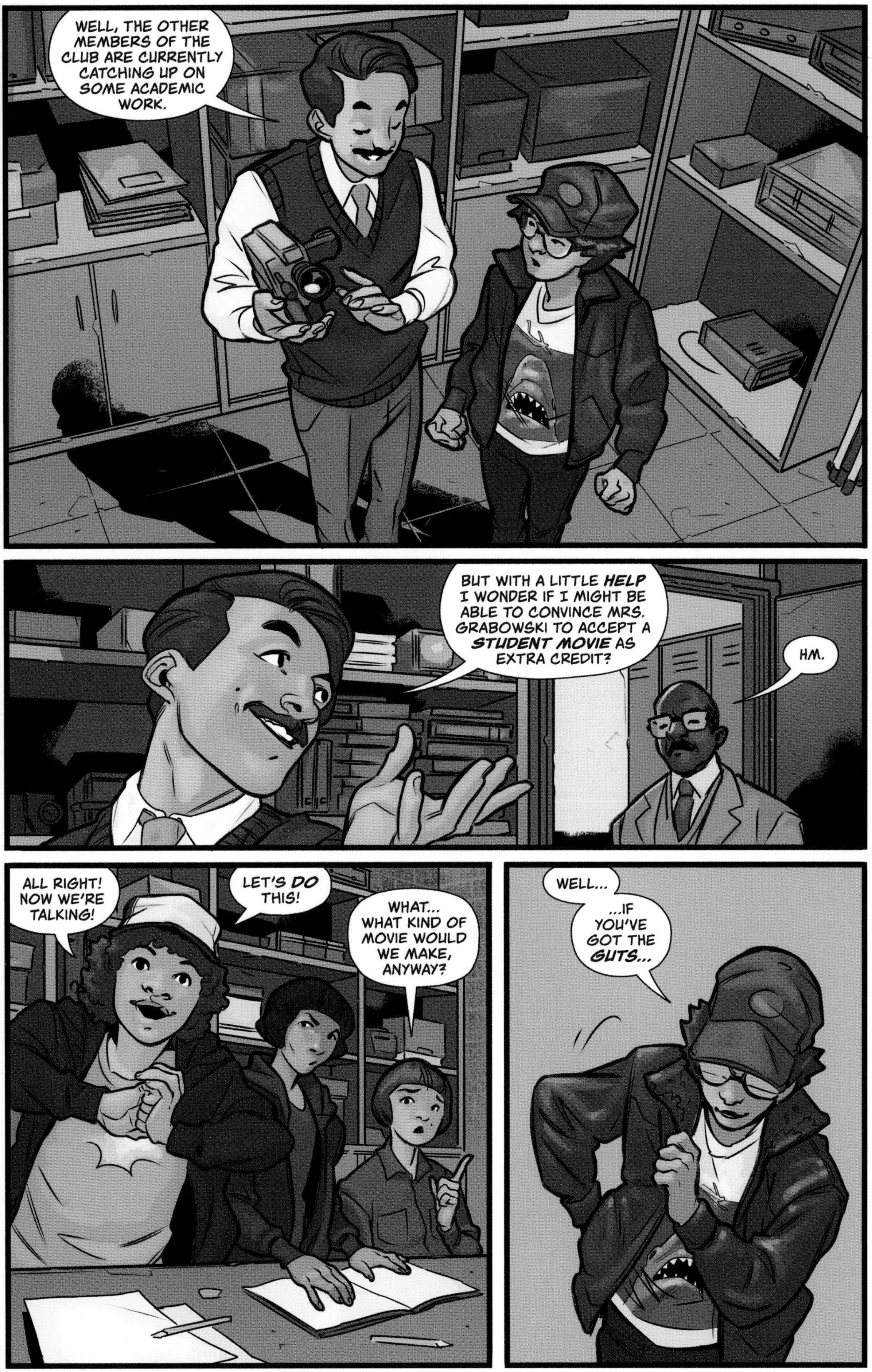
WELL, THE OTHER MEMBERS OF THE CLUB ARE CURRENTLY CATCHING UP ON SOME ACADEMIC WORK.
BUT WITH A LITTLE HELP I WONDER IF I MIGHT BE ABLE TO CONVINCE MRS. GRABOWSKI TO ACCEPT A STUDENT MOVIE AS EXTRA CREDIT?
HM.
ALL RIGHT! NOW WE'RE TALKING!
LET'S DO THIS!
WHAT... WHAT KIND OF MOVIE WOULD WE MAKE, ANYWAY?
WELL...
...IF YOU'VE GOT THE GUTS...

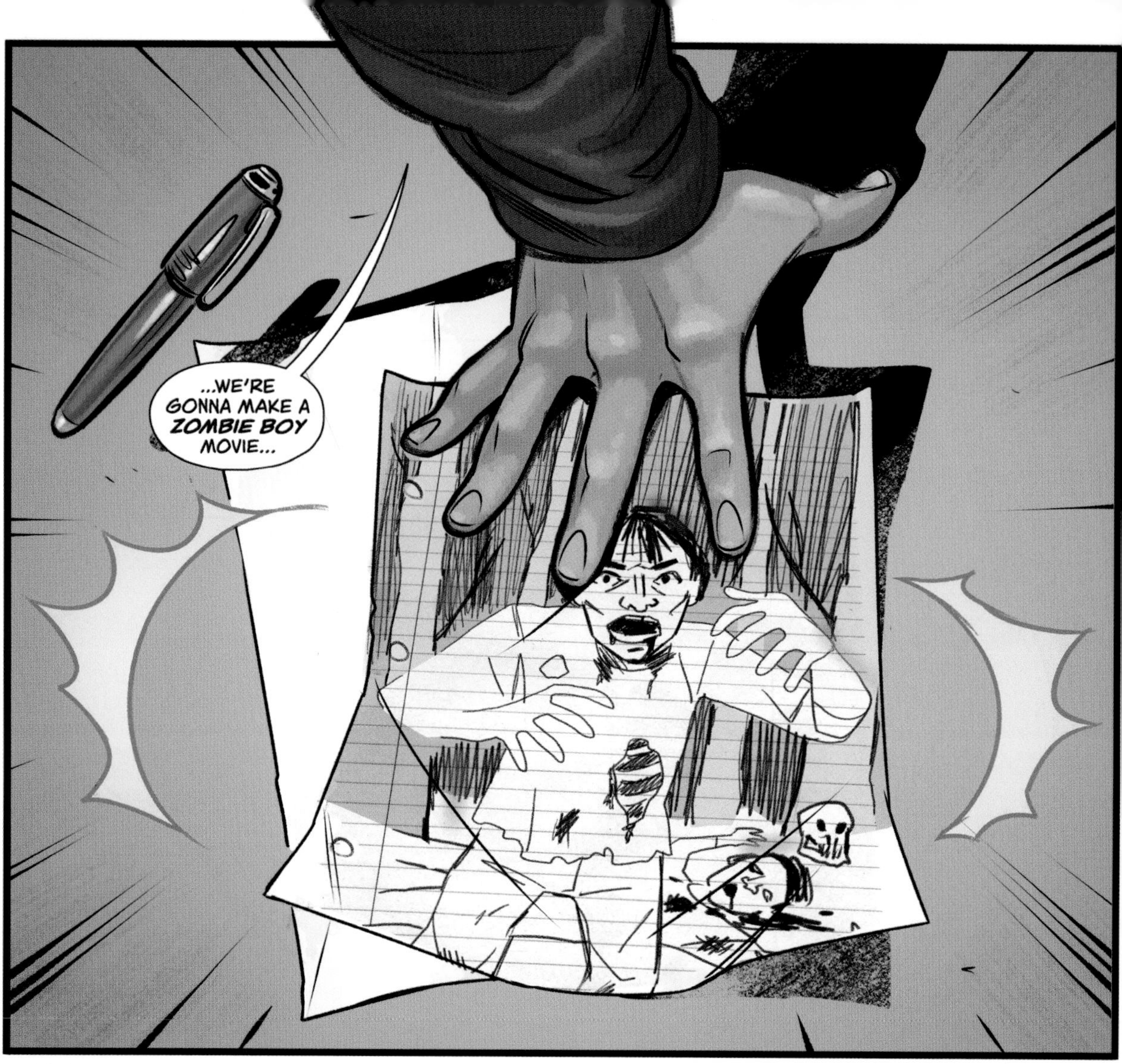
...WE'RE GONNA MAKE A ZOMBIE BOY MOVIE...

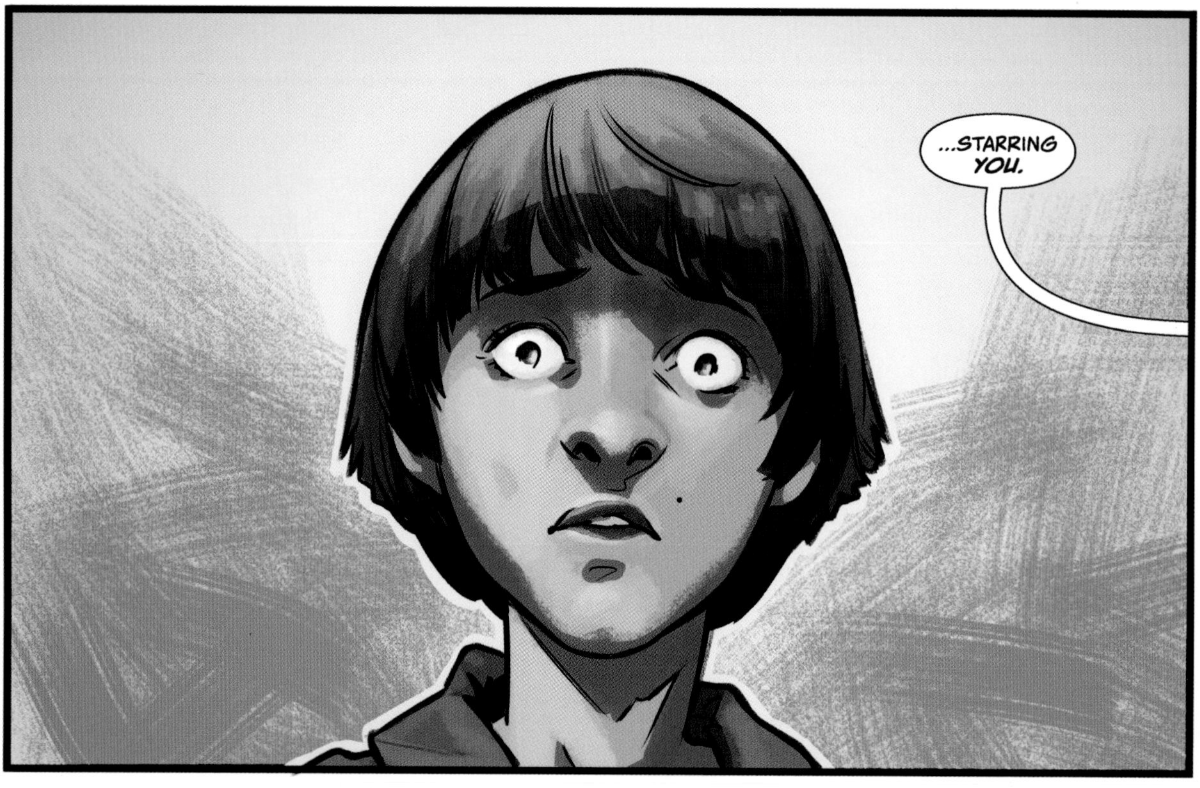
...STARRING YOU.

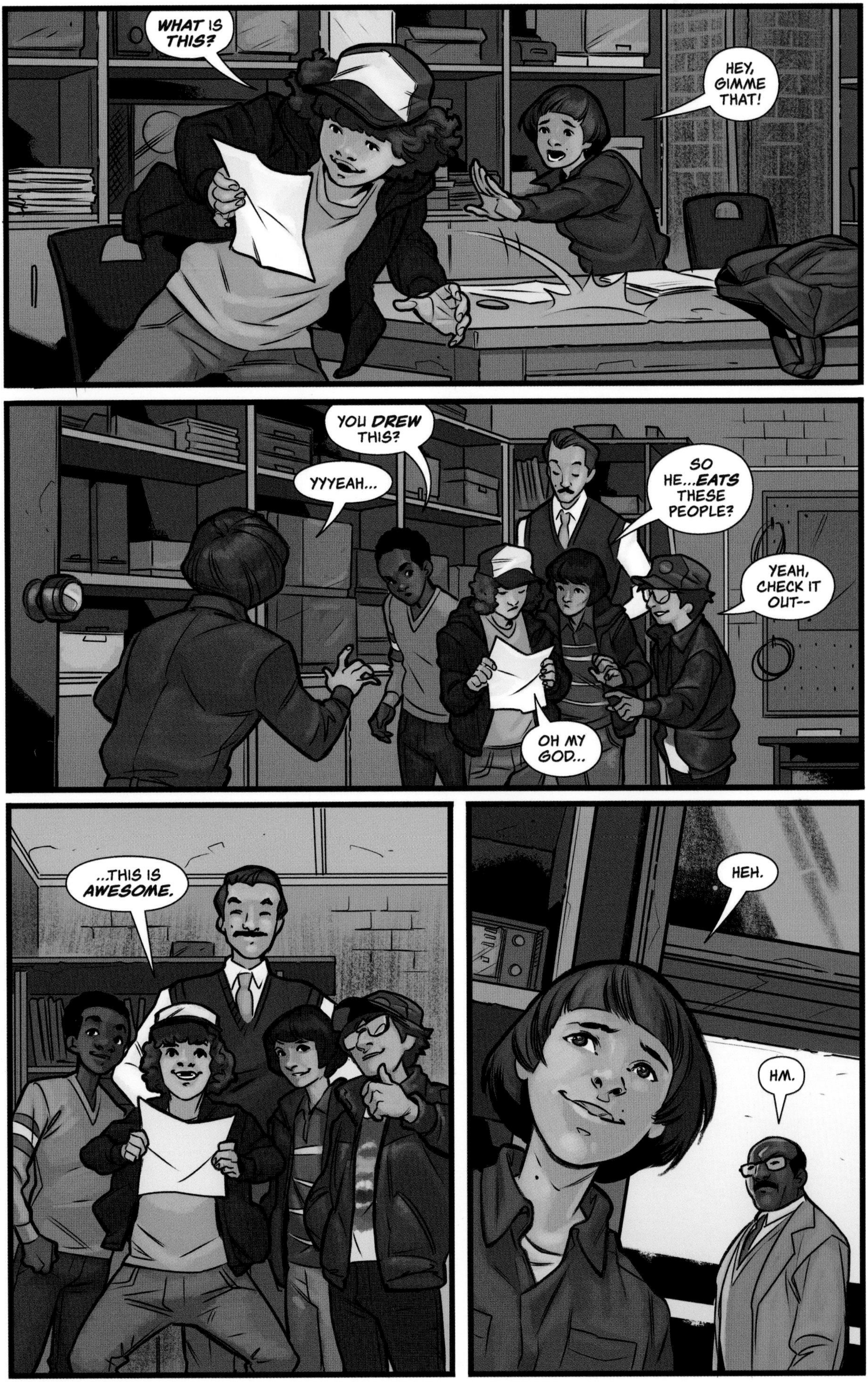
WHAT IS THIS?
HEY, GIMME THAT!
YOU DREW THIS?
YYYEAH...
SO HE...EATS THESE PEOPLE?
YEAH, CHECK IT OUT--
OH MY GOD...
...THIS IS AWESOME.
HEH.
HM.

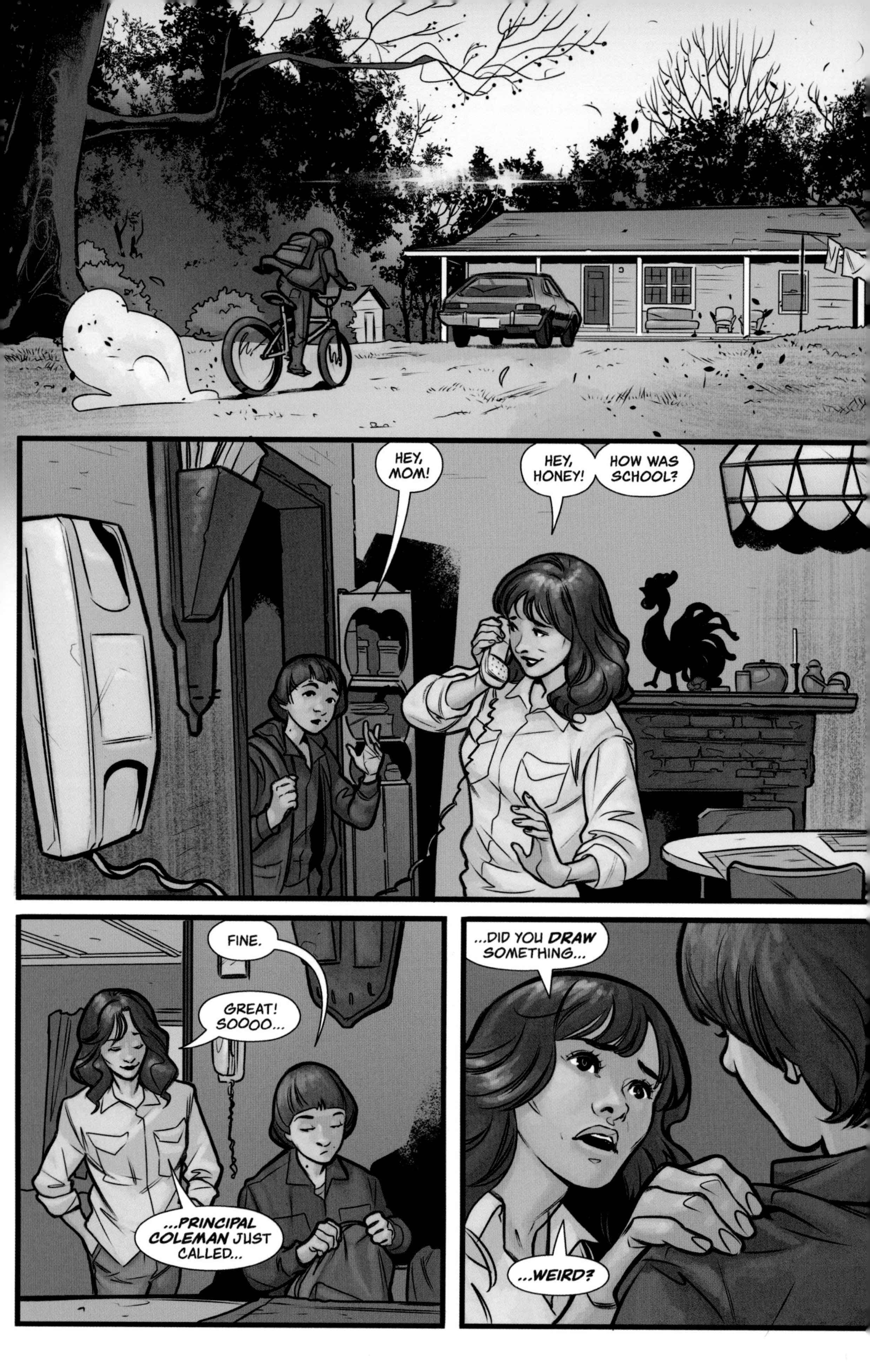
HEY, MOM!
HEY, HONEY!
HOW WAS SCHOOL?
FINE.
GREAT! SOOOO...
...PRINCIPAL COLEMAN JUST CALLED...
...DID YOU DRAW SOMETHING...
...WEIRD?

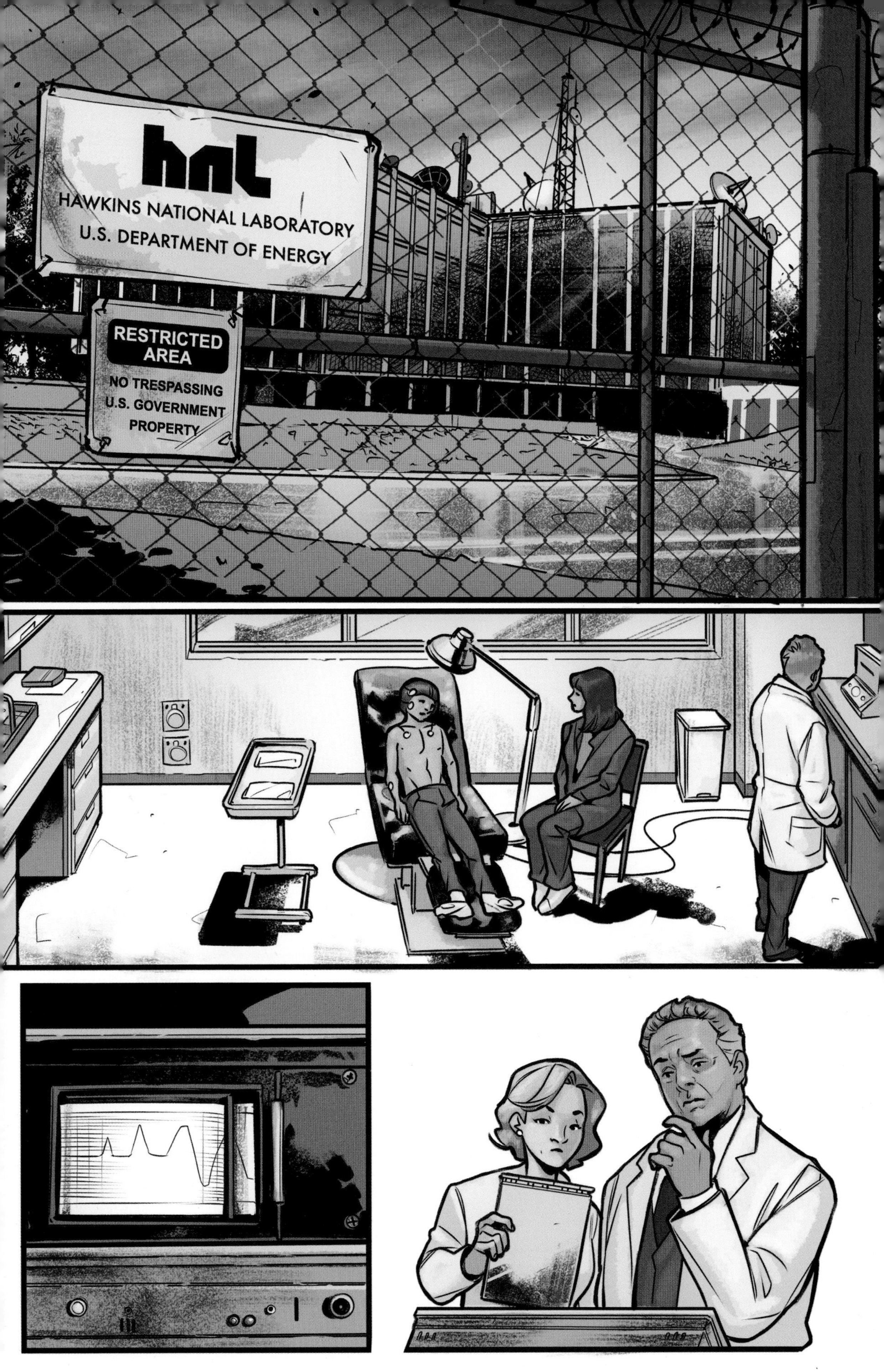
hnl
HAWKINS NATIONAL LABORATORY
U.S. DEPARTMENT OF ENERGY
RESTRICTED AREA
NO TRESPASSING
U.S. GOVERNMENT PROPERTY

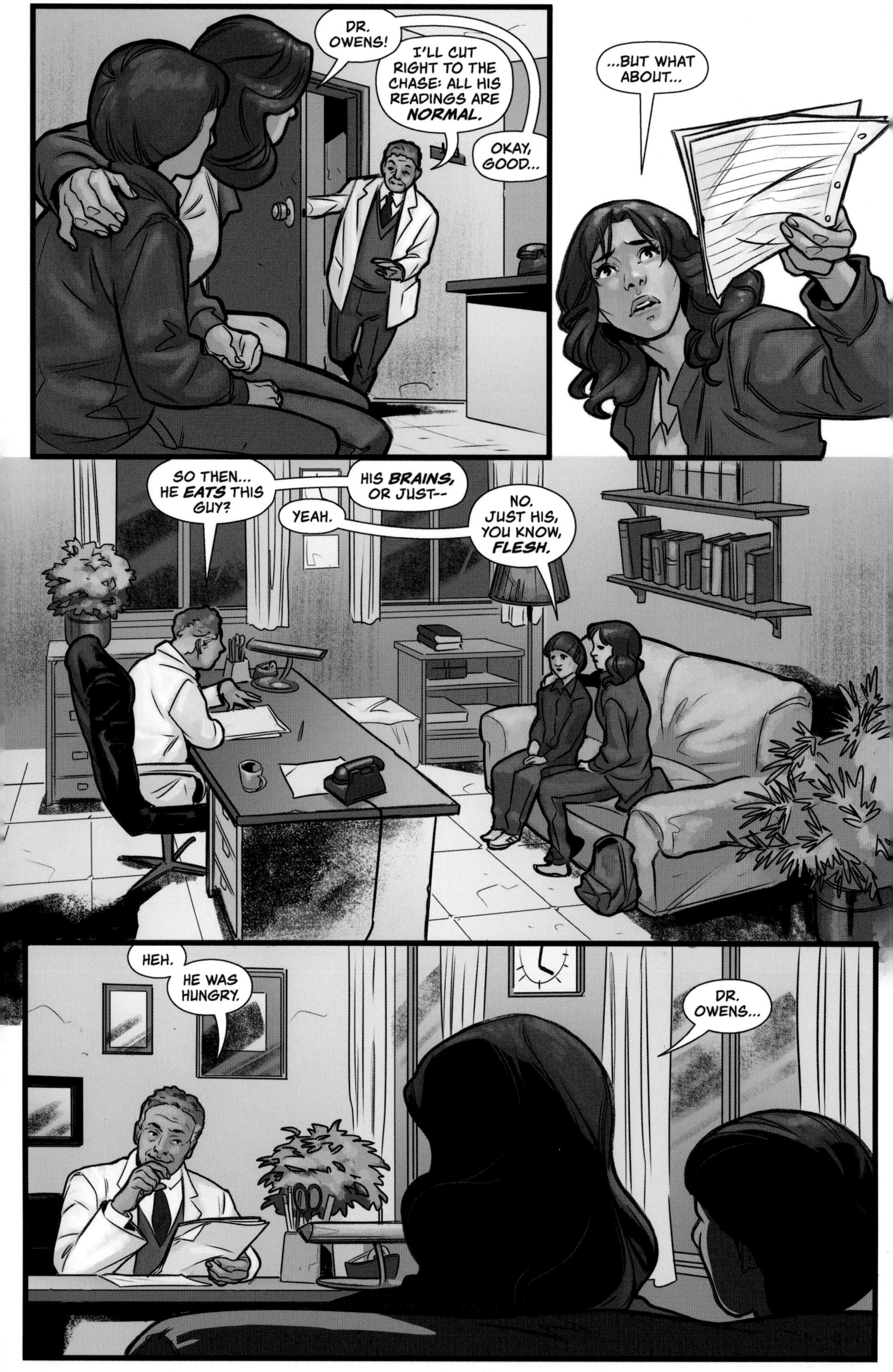
DR. OWENS!
I'LL CUT RIGHT TO THE CHASE: ALL HIS READINGS ARE NORMAL.
OKAY, GOOD...
...BUT WHAT ABOUT...
SO THEN... HE EATS THIS GUY?
YEAH.
HIS BRAINS, OR JUST--
NO. JUST HIS, YOU KNOW, FLESH.
HEH.
HE WAS HUNGRY.
DR. OWENS...

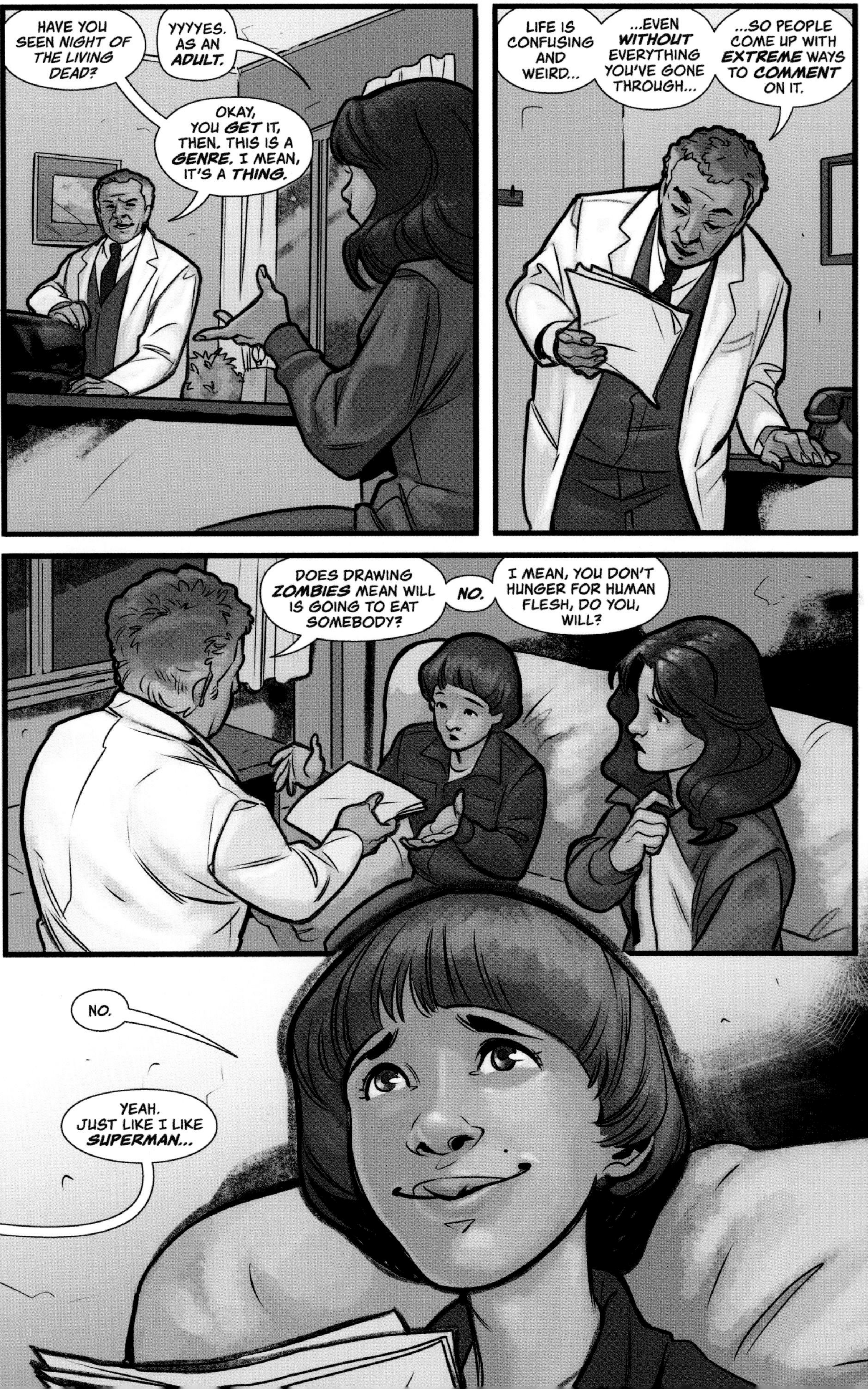
HAVE YOU SEEN NIGHT OF THE LIVING DEAD?
YYYYES. AS AN ADULT.
OKAY, YOU GET IT, THEN. THIS IS A GENRE. I MEAN, IT'S A THING.
LIFE IS CONFUSING AND WEIRD...
...EVEN WITHOUT EVERYTHING YOU'VE GONE THROUGH...
...SO PEOPLE COME UP WITH EXTREME WAYS TO COMMENT ON IT.
DOES DRAWING ZOMBIES MEAN WILL IS GOING TO EAT SOMEBODY?
NO.
I MEAN, YOU DON'T HUNGER FOR HUMAN FLESH, DO YOU, WILL?
NO.
YEAH. JUST LIKE I LIKE SUPERMAN...

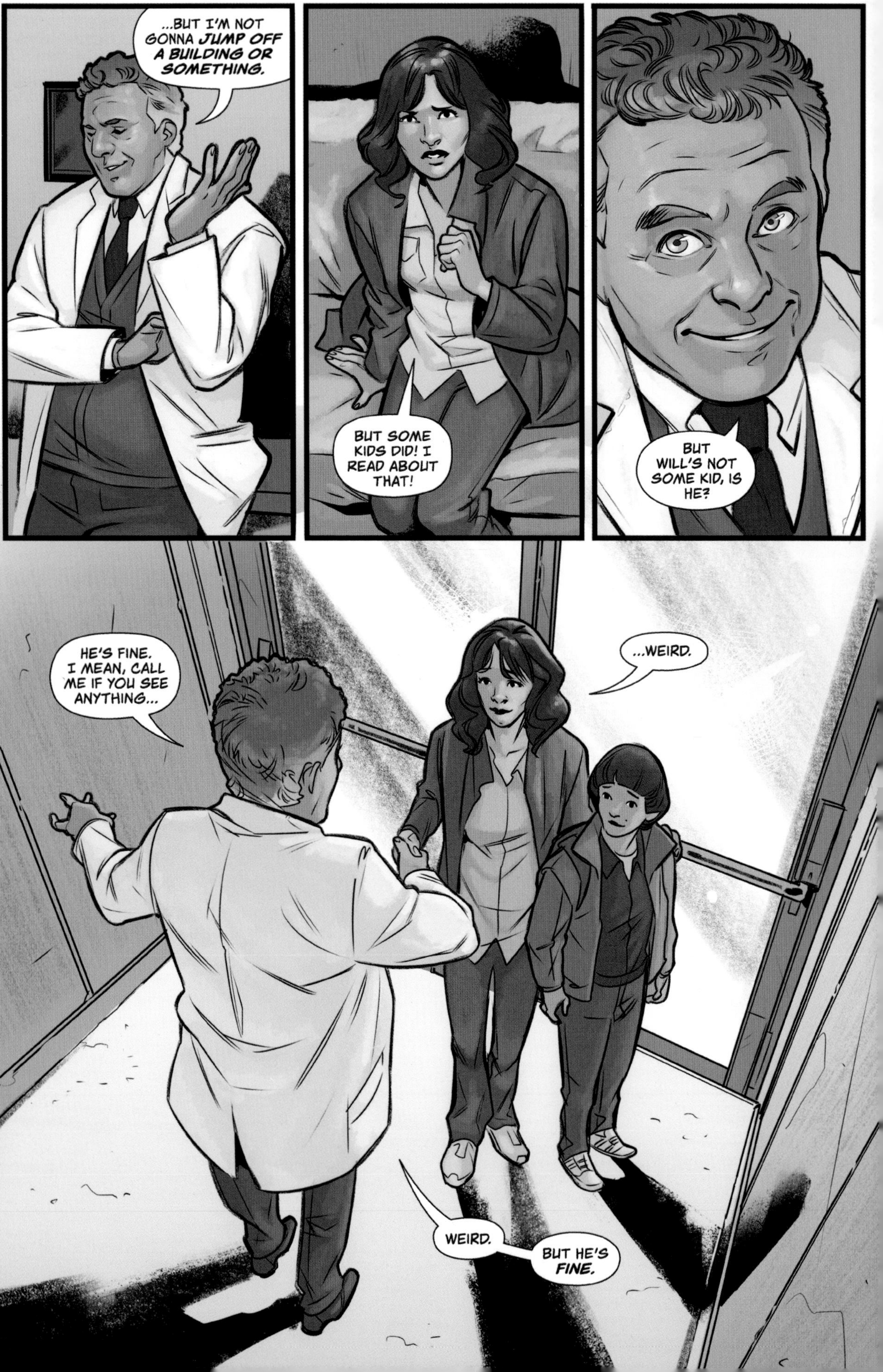
...BUT I'M NOT GONNA JUMP OFF A BUILDING OR SOMETHING.
BUT SOME KIDS DID! I READ ABOUT THAT!
BUT WILL'S NOT SOME KID, IS HE?
HE'S FINE. I MEAN, CALL ME IF YOU SEE ANYTHING...
...WEIRD.
WEIRD.
BUT HE'S FINE.

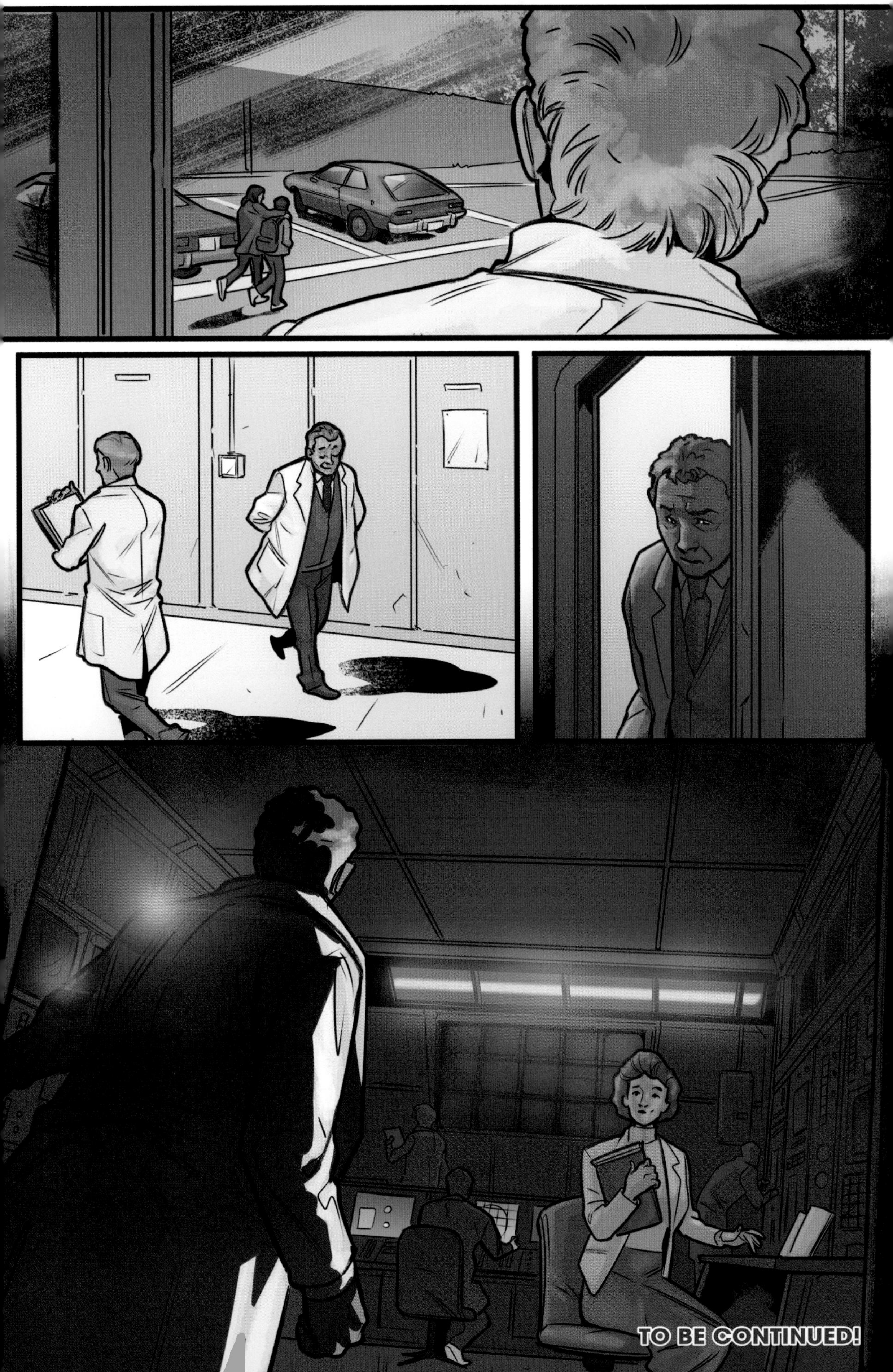
TO BE CONTINUED!

STRANGER THINGS

COLLECT THEM ALL!

Set of 12 Hardcover Books ISBN: 978-1-0982-5070-6

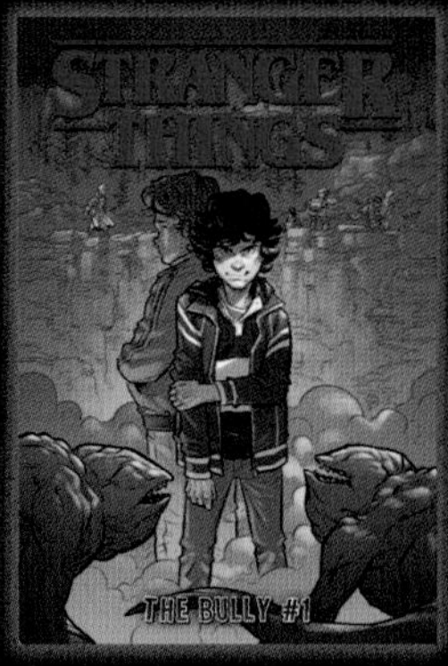
STRANGER THINGS
THE BULLY #1

Hardcover Book ISBN
978-1-0982-5071-3

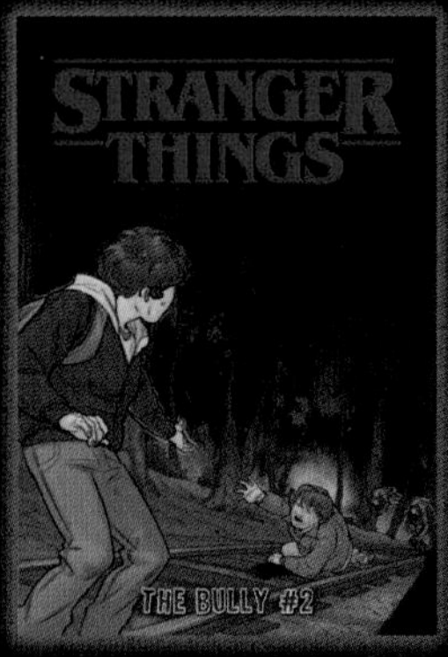
STRANGER THINGS
THE BULLY #2

Hardcover Book ISBN
978-1-0982-5072-0

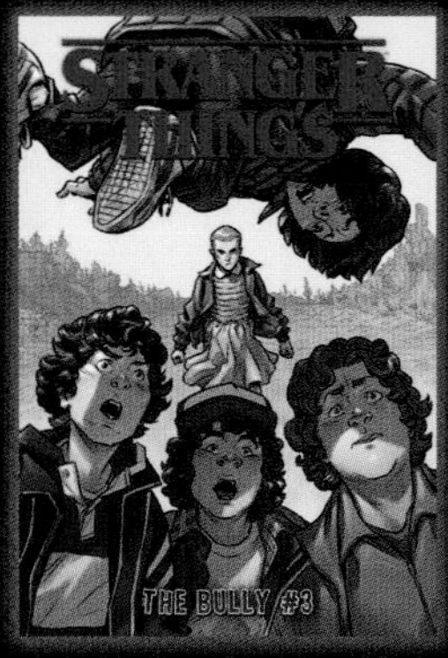
STRANGER THINGS
THE BULLY #3

Hardcover Book ISBN
978-1-0982-5073-7

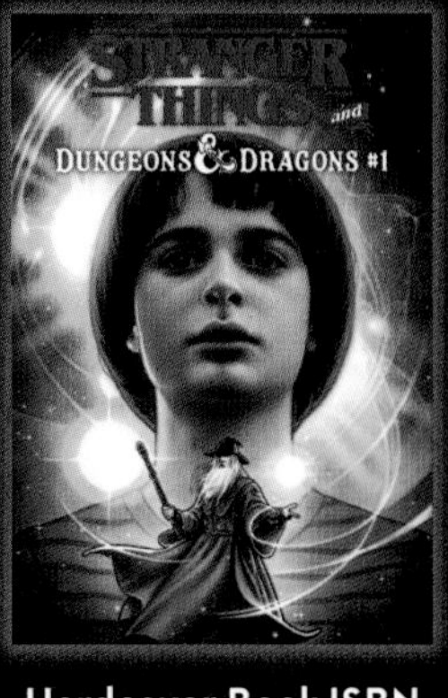
STRANGER THINGS and
DUNGEONS & DRAGONS #1

Hardcover Book ISBN
978-1-0982-5074-4

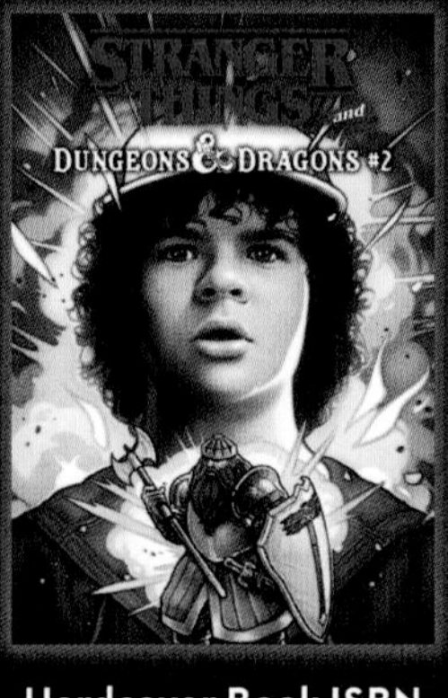
STRANGER THINGS and
DUNGEONS & DRAGONS #2

Hardcover Book ISBN
978-1-0982-5075-1

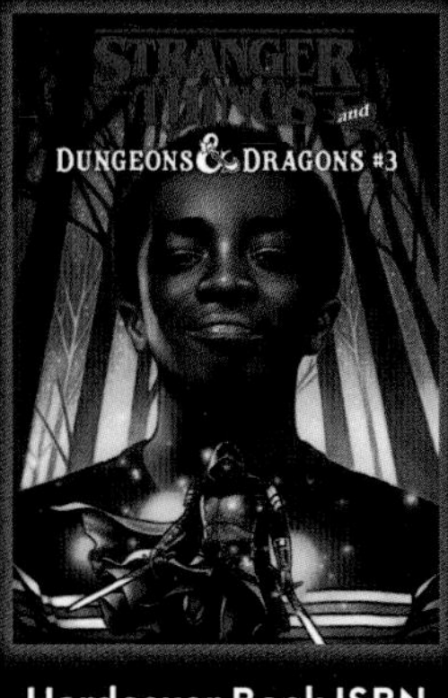
STRANGER THINGS and
DUNGEONS & DRAGONS #3

Hardcover Book ISBN
978-1-0982-5076-8

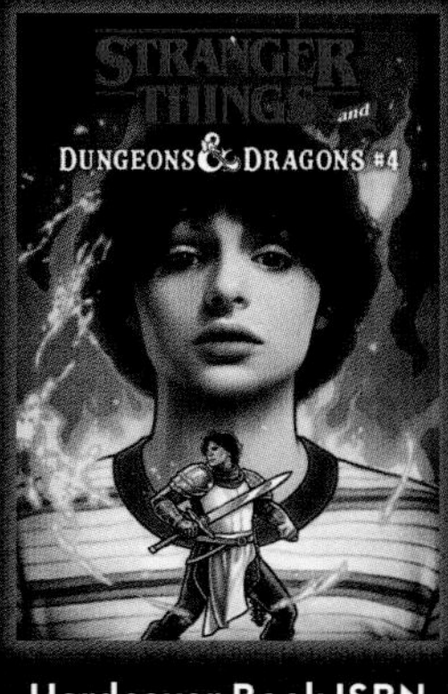
STRANGER THINGS and
DUNGEONS & DRAGONS #4

Hardcover Book ISBN
978-1-0982-5077-5

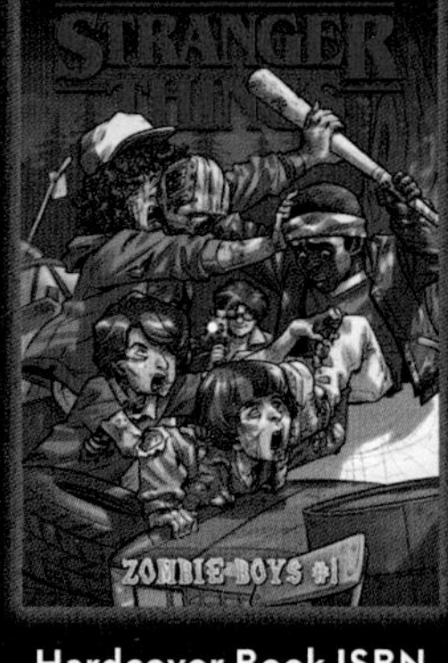
STRANGER THINGS
ZOMBIE BOYS #1

Hardcover Book ISBN
978-1-0982-5078-2

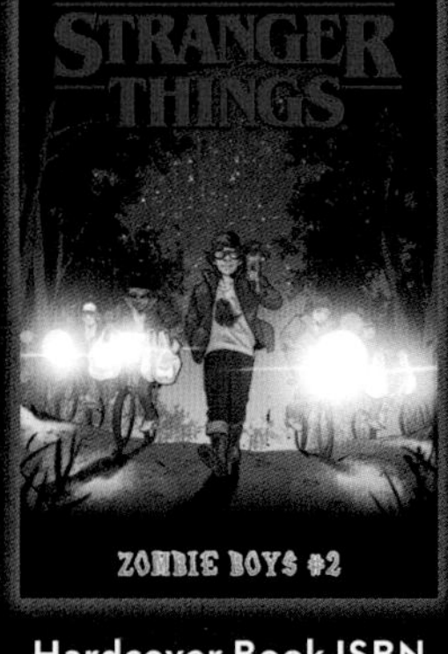
STRANGER THINGS
ZOMBIE BOYS #2

Hardcover Book ISBN
978-1-0982-5079-9

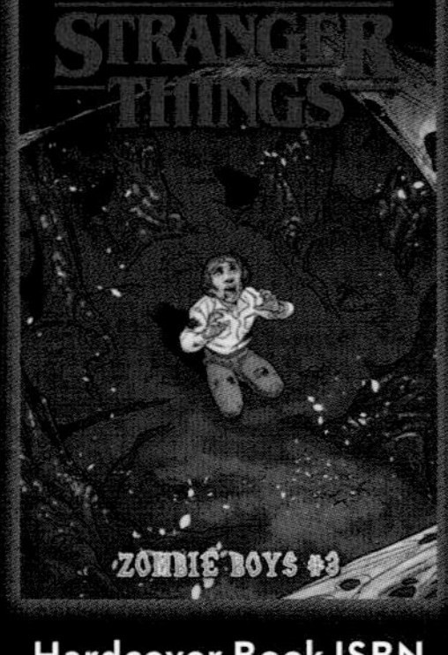
STRANGER THINGS
ZOMBIE BOYS #3

Hardcover Book ISBN
978-1-0982-5080-5